LONG SHADOWS

For many years, Colonel Robert Farrance has lived a respectable life. Nobody knows that his present prosperity is founded upon his earlier life as a ruthless and determined bandit. Then a figure from his past arrives in town, threatening to expose his history — and asking Farrance to assist him in securing his lost proceeds from a long-ago train robbery. The colonel acquiesces. But triumph looks to turn to tragedy when Farrance stands to lose all that he holds most precious . . .

CLYDE BARKER

LONG SHADOWS

Complete and Unabridged

LINFORD
Leicester

First published in Great Britain in 2014 by
Robert Hale Limited
London

First Linford Edition
published 2016
by arrangement with
Robert Hale
an imprint of The Crowood Press
Wiltshire

*A catalogue record for this book is available
from the British Library.*

ISBN 978–1–4448–3074–3

Published by
F. A. Thorpe (Publishing)
Anstey, Leicestershire

Set by Words & Graphics Ltd.
Anstey, Leicestershire
Printed and bound in Great Britain by
T. J. International Ltd., Padstow, Cornwall

This book is printed on acid-free paper

1

On a pleasant summer's evening in early June, 1891, Colonel Robert Farrance was going through some business papers in the library of his house. In the paddock at the back of the house, his sixteen-year-old daughter was putting her pony through its paces and it lacked only twenty minutes until the gong would sound to announce the evening meal. All in all, Farrance was a man who felt that the world was treating him pretty well. He signed the last of the documents and then got up and wandered over to the window to watch his daughter trying to master the art of riding side-saddle.

At sixty-three years of age, Robert Farrance was still in remarkable shape, both mentally and physically. He might have been one of the wealthiest men in the county, but he had not let himself go to seed by eating, drinking and smoking more than was good for him — the way men often did at that age when they had a little money to spare. Nor had he allowed his health to deteriorate by failing to get sufficient exercise. It was his proud boast that he weighed the same now as he had done when he was twenty.

As he stood at the window and gazed out across the many acres of land adjoining the house, *his* land, Farrance revelled in that deep satisfaction that comes from the knowledge that you are somebody of account. Not just here in the little town of Whyteleafe, either; his influence and business contacts stretched all the way to Pittsburgh and beyond.

There was a soft tap at the door.

'Come in,' said Farrance and his housekeeper entered the room, an apologetic look upon her face.

'I'm so sorry to disturb you, sir. There's a vagrant come calling at the kitchen door.'

'A vagrant? Well of course, Mrs Thomas. Give him a meal and some food to take away, too.' Robert Farrance's generosity to hobos and down-and-outs was legendary in Whyteleafe.

'It's not a meal that he wants, sir. He wants to see you in person. In fact, he says that he is an old friend.'

'You're sure that this isn't some acquaintance of mine looking a little rough because he has been on a hunting trip or something of that kind?'

'Oh no, sir,' said Mrs Thomas, looking faintly shocked that the colonel could even think that she would not recognize a gentleman when she met one, no matter what he was wearing. 'It's not just his clothes, sir, begging your pardon. He is somebody who has been living out in the open for more than just a week or two. I wondered if you wanted me to get a couple of the men to send him on his way if he was troublesome?'

Colonel Farrance was in a good humour that afternoon and inclined to be Christian towards a fellow being less fortunate than himself. To his housekeeper's immense surprise, he said, 'Show him up here, Mrs Thomas.'

'Show him up, sir? He's a dirty, ragged fellow. Would it not be more fitting were you to come down and interview him in the kitchen?'

Farrance laughed. 'No, no. He's a man and doubtless a sinner, just as I am. Let him come up here. Who knows, I might even be able to find some employment for him. I feel in the mood to share the blessings which providence has seen fit to bestow upon me.'

'Just as you say, sir,' said Mrs Thomas dubiously.

A few minutes later, there came another knock upon the door to the library and the housekeeper brought into the room the scruffiest, dirtiest man that the colonel had seen in a good long while. He was dressed in an outfit which might have been filched from a scarecrow and was filthy-dirty as well. Although he looked to be no older than

Colonel Farrance, his face told of a more arduous life entirely. To complete the unfavourable impression, one of his eyes was covered with an eyepatch, giving him the aspect of a pirate or freebooter.

'All right, Mrs Thomas,' said the colonel. 'You may leave us now.' After she had left the room, not without misgivings and with some shaking of the head and muttering of disapproving clucks, Farrance said to the man, 'Well, you represented yourself to my housekeeper as an old friend. Your appearance calls nobody to mind, but perhaps your name will jog my memory. I don't think I caught it.'

'My name? It is Wilson. Ikey Wilson.'

At these words, Colonel Farrance felt as though he had received a sudden blow to the pit of his stomach or perhaps taken a bullet through the heart. 'Ikey Wilson? Where did you hear that name? If this is some attempt at blackmail, then you have chosen the wrong person to play it upon. Ikey

Wilson has been dead these thirty years or more.' He strode across the room to the bell-pull. 'I'm more than half minded to ring for assistance and have you pitched out into the highway. You're a rare scoundrel coming here with such a tale!'

The man seemed to be unmoved by this threat. His face displayed a look of quizzical amusement and he said, 'Dead, am I, hey? You surprise me, Bob.'

So long had it been since anybody had ventured to address Farrance by the diminutive in this way, that he was taken aback. The ragged figure in front of him continued, 'Yes, 'Long Bob' Farrance. I never thought to set eyes upon you again, but I am right glad that I have done so. I reckon you owe me. Were it not for me and others, you would have hanged back in 1861.'

Farrance walked right up to the man and stared hard into his face. He said, 'If you are really Ikey Wilson, Mad Ikey as he was known, then you will have a scar on your upper arm. Show it me and tell how you came by it.'

The man grinned and rolled up the sleeve of his shirt to reveal a grimy arm, across the bicep of which was a raised, red weal. 'Caught a bullet getting away from that bank in Colorado. There were five of us that day. Want me to name them?'

At the realization that this man really was who he claimed to be, Colonel Farrance almost staggered in shock. For over thirty years, he had lived an honest, upright and God-fearing life and now this!

'Well?' said the man. 'You believe me now? You know that I am Ikey Wilson, your comrade from the old days. The good old days, as you might say.'

Farrance went over to a cabinet and poured himself a whiskey. Then he poured out another glass and took it over to where Wilson was standing. 'Come and sit down here,' he said, 'and tell me what you want of me and how come you are not dead.'

The two men went over to the desk and pulled up chairs. Wilson sipped his drink appreciatively, marshalling his thoughts. Then he began to speak.

'You recollect how we was in Fort Tyler at the back end of 1860? You, me, Andrew Crawley and a few others?'

'Yes, I recall it vividly,' said Farrance, his face drawn and grim.

'We got into a fight at the faro table and you shot that fellow. Then there was an almighty row and somehow in all the confusion, you were caught and we got away. Anyways, there was a posse of men took you for trial in Evansville. There were too many of them, we could not get nigh to you. We thought at first they was going to lynch you, but you got a fair trial and was lodged in the gaol until they could hang you. You remember all that?'

'I am not apt to forget,' said the colonel. 'You kind of tend to remember it when you look out of your cell window and see a gallows waiting for you.'

'Well then, you likewise know what

chanced next, which is to say the whole gang of us busting into that gaol and freeing you. That was hot fighting, let me tell you.'

Colonel Farrance had a faraway look in his eyes. He had not brought these incidents to his mind for at least a decade or more. He said, 'You were mighty young then. I do not believe that you could have been above eighteen years of age.'

'I was seventeen,' said Wilson. 'Anyway, in all the excitement, I got myself shot. There was blood everywhere and you all thought that it was up with me. So amid all the banging and shouting and shooting, you and the others left me laying there outside the gaol and made off without me.'

'Which was badly done of us. We should have taken care to see if we could help you.'

'I was only a youngster. Happen you figured that I was no great loss.'

'No, it was nothing of the sort. There was so much smoke and firing and confusion. We never heard of you again. You can't blame us for thinking you were dead.'

'I ain't here to blame anybody for nothing. That's nothing to the purpose. I got away in the end, although no thanks to you fellows.'

Farrance stood up and went over to the window. Charlotte had finished her riding lesson and would like as not be coming to see him at any moment. No sooner had he thought this, than there was a rap at the door and without waiting to be invited in, the door burst open and his daughter rushed in. She began to speak, but then noticed the presence of another person and stopped herself. 'Sorry, Daddy, I didn't know you had company.'

'That's all right,' said the colonel. 'Tell Mrs Thomas not to bother with setting a place at table for me. Tell her I would be obliged if she could send up a tray for me and my friend here.'

The girl left, puzzled and a little uneasy. As she left the room, she gave

Ikey Wilson a long stare, obviously wondering what such an unkempt and ill-favoured fellow was doing in her father's inner sanctum. After she had gone, Wilson said, 'She seems like a right nice girl. Tell me now, does she know how you used to make your living?'

Farrance was across the room in the merest fraction of a second. He hauled Wilson to his feet and then slammed him against the wall with enough force to set the man's ears ringing. In a soft and deadly voice he said, 'Do not set mind to my family, Wilson. Do not even think of them. Anybody touches them or causes them even the slightest uneasiness and I will take that person and kill him like a dog. Is that plain?'

Ikey Wilson did not appear to be in the least bit perturbed by this sudden outburst of violence. He said in the same cool, level voice, 'Still got that famous temper of yours, I see. It was not really your family I wished to see, Bob. It was you.'

The colonel released Wilson and went over to the cabinet to pour them both another drink. He said, 'You best tell me the play. You are right, I still have a temper and it has stood me in good stead. I do not think that you would want to get crosswise to me.'

'Nobody's going to get crosswise to anybody, or so I hope. I need your help, is all.'

'How did you find me after all these years? You have not been searching these last thirty years, I suppose?'

Wilson laughed. 'Not hardly. I heard your name by chance as I was passing through. I hung around long enough to sneak a look at you and be sure you were the same man and then here I am.'

'Yes,' said Farrance, 'and here you are. This is where the knife meets the bone, as we say in these parts. What do you want of me? If it's anything in the blackmailing line, I tell you now you are plumb out of luck. If you want a sum of money to set yourself up somewhere, well, that may be possible to arrange.'

Wilson laughed again. 'You are not in much of a position to dictate to me. I reckon that that sentence of death still holds good, even after all these years. Suppose I reported your whereabouts to the authorities in Evansville?'

'So it *is* blackmail. We shall see about this.'

'Lord, you are as hasty as ever you was, Bob. I am not blackmailing you. Nor do I want any of your money. I am here to ask for your help.'

'If you don't want money, then what is it you are after?'

'I didn't say that I don't want money. I said I didn't want your money.'

'Well whose, then? And why do you think I will help you?'

At this point, Mrs Thomas arrived, accompanied by one of the staff and bearing trays of hot food. After this had been set down, she said to her master, 'Is everything quite all right, sir? You don't need anything else?'

'No, thank you, Mrs Thomas. We are fine here. Thank you.'

After the woman had left, Ikey Wilson said, 'She thinks that I am a bad man and can't make out why you are entertaining me here.'

'What is this help you want of me?'

'Time was,' said Wilson in a thoughtful tone of voice, 'time was when 'Long Bob' Farrance and his boys were the terror of three states. They went after stages, trains, banks and anywhere else where there was money to be had. I was flattered when you let me join the gang when I was no more than a kid. Me, seventeen years of age and riding with the most dangerous set of desperados you ever heard tell of.'

'We were all a good deal younger in those days.'

'Isn't that the truth! I joined the army soon after that business at Evansville and stayed in it to 1865. That's how I lost this eye. Then, after the war I set up as a road agent and did some business in different lines. You know. Cowboy, barkeep, cardsharp. All manner of things. Then about ten years after the surrender, who do you think I met up with?'

'I couldn't guess,' said Farrance. 'You know, you are a wordy and talkative fellow, Ikey. I suppose that you will reach your point this side of Christmas?'

'You will have your joke. Well, it was Andrew Crawley.'

'Was it, by God? And what did you get up to with that skunk?'

'Yes, he told me that you and he had had somewhat of a falling out.'

'That,' said Colonel Farrance, 'is one way of putting the case.'

'Me and him teamed up and we rode together for some years. Sometimes just us, other times with a group of fellows.'

'Just like the old days, you mean, when we were all on the scout together.'

Wilson, who had been sitting at his ease in the colonel's favourite chair, now got up and began pacing to and fro. He had been pretty relaxed when talking of being left for dead in Evansville, but whatever he was about to relate now was making him decidedly agitated.

'You want another drink?' asked Farrance.

'Maybe later. I want to tell my tale first. It came to a time in 1879 when me and Crawley and some others took it into our head to take a train. This was up Kansas way. We stopped it at night, as it toiled up a slope. You know the trick, waving a red lantern to warn of danger.'

'I have heard of such tricks,' said Colonel Farrance drily.

'You surely have,' said Ikey Wilson. 'Did we but know it, we had hit the big prize with this one. It was loaded down with gold from back west. Enough to make all of us rich. All eight of us. Things went wrong once we had loaded up our horses with the gold and made to ride off. Some of those damned passengers took it into their heads to start shooting at us once we were off the train. You know how it is sometimes when that happens. The long and the short of it was that me and Andrew Crawley both made off with enough gold to keep us comfortably without working for the rest of our days.'

'So you were well set up in 1879? What went wrong? You gamble it all away?'

'Gamble, nothing! What went wrong was that I got caught and Crawley sent word that he would take care of my share of the gold. We both had the gold loaded up in saddle-bags and as soon as he caught sight of my predicament, why he just lit out of there with both his horse and mine. A double share, as it were, of the profits from that robbery. He bought a ranch and settled down until he is as wealthy and respectable now as you look to be.

'I drew ten years for robbery. Served every single day with another year thrown in for attacking a guard one time. Never opened my mouth about any of the others.'

'When did you get out?'

'Six months since. I went straight to Crawley's place and asked him to act honourable and hand over half of his wealth. He could not have bought that place without using my money as well.'

'What did he say?' asked Farrance.

'He laughed at me. Laughed at me and then got a couple of his men to rough me up and throw me out.'

'And then?'

'What do you mean, then? Then, nothing. I have no money, only the rags on my back. I have been sleeping out and moving around. Until yesterday, when I heard tell of your name, that is.'

Farrance got to his feet as well. He said, 'And you want my help in getting your treasure from Andrew Crawley, is that how the land lies?'

'That's it, Bob. You owe me. If not for me and the other boys, you woulda hung thirty years back. You cannot deny it.'

'Don't crowd me, I won't have it. Suppose I gave you some money, would that meet the case?'

'I don't want charity. I want only what is mine.'

The colonel could not help but smile at this, which irked Wilson, because he said, 'What the hell are you smiling about? You think this is funny?'

'No, I don't think it is funny. I was just smiling to hear you say that you want what is yours, in reference to some gold that you stole.'

'That is kind of funny, I will allow,' said Wilson. 'The point is, will you help me as I once helped you? There is a debt there to be paid.'

Colonel Farrance thought about it for a spell and then said slowly, 'Now I come to consider the case, I have a crow to pluck with Andrew Crawley myself. And you are right, I do owe you. But I do this as an act of honour, not because I am afeared of anything you may say to anybody about my past. I want that to be understood.'

'Hell, I know that. So it is a deal?'

Farrance walked over to the other man and put out his hand. 'Yes,' he said. 'It is a deal.'

2

After being freed from gaol on the eve of his execution, 'Long Bob' Farrance resolved that he could not continue in that way of life much longer. The prospect of facing a public hanging can have a powerful effect on a man and often causes him to review his life and reflect upon what has led him to such a pass. 'Long Bob' had amassed a considerable sum of money which was deposited in a safe and trustworthy bank and once he was free again, he came to a decision about his future. He said nothing of this to the members of the gang of which he was the leader.

For some weeks after his release from the gaol at Evansville, Farrance carried on in his usual way. Then one day in March, 1861, he simply vanished, leaving his old gang rudderless. He felt that it was a scurvy trick to play on such a loyal band, but when all was said and done, he had had enough of the outlaw life. Two weeks later came the shelling of Fort Sumter, followed by President Lincoln's call for volunteers. He had for a time in his youth been a West Pointer and so was able to secure a commission. Before he enlisted, Bob Farrance invested his money in various places. On an impulse, he put the bulk of it into factories in the north. Four years later, the war between the states was over and 'Long Bob' Farrance, the outlaw, had become Colonel Robert Farrance, the war hero.

After his discharge from the army, Farrance discovered to his amazement that he was a very wealthy man. His investments had all prospered and the products of the factories in which he had put his money were in great demand. Money makes money and as the years passed, Colonel Farrance just grew richer and richer.

So it came to pass that by 1891, the one-time outlaw and former war hero was living the life of a gentleman of leisure, with nothing more pressing to do with his time than keep an eye upon the various enterprises in which he now had a controlling interest. The unexpected arrival of 'Mad Ikey' Wilson came as a bolt from the blue.

After agreeing to help Wilson in his quest, Colonel Farrance began making the necessary arrangements. He had a room prepared for Wilson and also ordered the bath to be filled. By the time that he had bathed, shaved and been dressed in some old clothes belonging to one of his staff, Wilson looked a different man. He was still quite unmistakably a rough and ready sort of fellow and not any sort of a gentleman, but at least he no longer looked like a scarecrow.

Charlotte was consumed by curiosity about the visitor. She bearded her father in his library while Ikey Wilson was engaged in making himself more presentable.

'Who is he, Daddy?' she asked. 'He

looks like a pirate.'

'He is an old acquaintance of mine from before the war,' said Farrance. 'He will be staying with us for a few days and then I am going on a short journey with him.'

'Well, I don't like him!' the girl declared. 'He smells awful and looks like he crawled out from under a log.'

'Don't be a snob, miss,' Farrance said sharply. 'It is not what I have raised you to. He is down on his luck and I am aiming to help set him back upon his feet. I was not always the gentleman that you see before you now.'

'Will you be away long?' asked his daughter, a little chastened by his tone.

'No, I hope not. Come here, child. I did not mean to snap at you.' The two of them embraced briefly and then the colonel said to her, 'While he is here, I would be obliged if you could be pleasant to Mr Wilson. I have not seen him since he was a boy and the years have not been kind to him.'

Ikey Wilson made every effort to

make himself agreeable to Charlotte and the servants. He was a witty man, with a dry sense of humour, and over the days that he stayed at the house, those who had contact with him gradually came to accept his presence there.

After breakfast on the day after Wilson had turned up at Farrance's place, the two men went up into the attic together. 'I have not set mind to guns nor any sort of weapon, these many years,' said Colonel Farrance. 'What I have in that line will be up here.'

'You have become a regular peace-maker in your later years,' said Wilson. 'Is that the way of it?'

'I have done enough shooting and killing both before and during the war to satisfy any man. I hope that we can accomplish your end without any bloodshed.'

They hauled out two large trunks, covered with cobwebs and dust. When once he had managed to overcome the rusty catches and succeeded in wrenching open the lids, a number of cloth-wrapped bundles were revealed to sight. Farrance lifted these out and placed them on the bare wooden boards of the attic floor. They proved to contain a number of guns of distinctly antiquated design. Ikey Wilson picked up one of the pistols and laughed. 'Lord God, Bob, you are surely not proposing to go after Andrew Crawley while armed only with a cap-and-ball revolver? We would be massacred.'

'I hope it will not come to gunplay and that we will be able to reason with the man. But you are right. Nothing here will do.'

The two of them tried out the actions of some of the other weapons, cocking and dry-firing them. The two muskets were also muzzle loaders and looked like the kind of thing you might come across in a museum. Wilson observed, 'You have surely fallen behind the times here. I have been locked up for eleven years and even I am more up to date than you on this subject.'

'That is as may be,' said Farrance. 'I guess that we might need to equip ourselves with firearms, just in case Crawley does not see eye to eye with us on this matter. We had best go into town this morning and see what we can find.'

'What is it between you and Crawley? When I picked up with him again, must have been 1875 or 1876, he said that you were after killing him when last you met. What was that about?'

'It does not signify. That is purely my affair. It is enough for you to know that I will help you obtain your justice from the man and that I am prepared to press the point if he will not see reason.'

'Happen that's all I need to know.'

'Yes,' said Farrance. 'Happen it is.'

There was enormous surprise when Colonel Robert Farrance walked into the gunsmith's shop in Whyteleafe and requested to look at a selection of the most up-to-date and modern weapons that they had to offer in that establishment. Such a thing had never been known before, the colonel never having been seen with a gun, even for hunting and suchlike. Some in town had him pegged for a Quaker or something of that sort.

'What can I do for you, Colonel Farrance?' asked the clerk obsequiously. 'It surely is a pleasure to serve a gentleman of your standing.'

'That's nothing to the purpose,' said Farrance brusquely. 'Me and my friend here want to look at some pistols. After that, we'll be wanting a rifle each.'

They were shown various pistols, mainly Colts, none of which appealed to Colonel Farrance. At length, he enquired, 'Have you no single-action weapons? I cannot be doing with these heavy trigger pulls to raise the hammer. It puts me off.'

'Single action? Well, sir, you are in luck today and no mistake! We have just had a consignment of the new Remington, the one that they started making last year. It is a beautiful weapon.' He went into the back room and returned with two pistols: one in blued steel and the other nickel-plated. 'There is not much call for single-action pistols now. I am surprised that Remington thought it worth producing these. They take the standard .44 centre-fire cartridge.'

Colonel Farrance picked up one of the pistols and hefted it in his hand. The grips were made of hard, black rubber, which felt a little strange, but otherwise it seemed all right. He cocked the piece a few times and the action was as smooth as silk.

Sensing that he had almost made a sale, the clerk said, 'These are five-and-a-half-inch barrels. We have the seven-and-a-half-inch version if that would be preferred?'

'Yes, let me see them, please.'

After some debate with Wilson, they left the shop with two of the nickel-plated Remingtons, both with long barrels, and two rifles. They also took with them enough ammunition to practise with the new guns before using them in action, if it came to that. After the gunsmith's, they visited another store, where two sets of stout, working man's clothes were ordered: one for Wilson and one for Farrance.

As the two men rode back to Colonel Farrance's spread, he remarked to Wilson, 'I never could be doing with a double-action pistol. By the time you've squeezed that trigger hard enough to raise the hammer, your aim is altogether spoiled. I like to be able to fire with just the merest twitch of my finger.'

'There is something in that,' said Wilson thoughtfully. 'Mind, if your aim is just to throw a lot of lead around in a hurry, then a double action is just the thing.'

'That's true enough, but I don't look to be engaging in any sort of gun battle. Mark what I say, I will assist you in your dealings with Crawley, but I am not going to take part in some private act of vengeance. This is purely business.'

'Strange that you should take that line,' said Wilson, 'seeing as how you so plainly hate the fellow. I would have thought you might be glad for a chance to shoot him.'

Farrance reined in his horse and turned to face the other man. 'I have told you once and for all, that is my affair. You need not refer to it again. What I have against Crawley is between me and him. It is not to be made the theme of general conversation.'

'Just as you say, Bob,' said Wilson equably.

Charlotte was practising the violin when they got back and Ikey Wilson stopped in the hallway to listen. He said to Colonel Farrance, 'She surely plays that instrument beautifully. You are lucky to have such a daughter. Tell me, how is it that I have not seen her mother?'

'Her mother is dead,' said Farrance shortly. 'She died in childbirth.'

'And so you raised the child by yourself? That is the hell of a thing. Did she go to school?'

'No, I hired teachers and tutors for whatever was needful.'

'I reckon you must feel some hatred to me. For breaking in upon such a peaceful life as this, I mean.'

As they walked towards the library, Farrance thought over what the other had said and when they were out of earshot of anybody else, he said, 'No, I don't feel any hatred for you, Ikey. I was not best pleased to see you turn up on my doorstep yesterday, but that is nothing. I knew at the time that we did wrong to run off out of Evansville without stopping to check if you were dead, wounded or what. I am not sorry to have a chance to put that right a little. I don't hate you.'

'It will be like the old times, the two of us on the scout and working together,' said Wilson. 'You might even enjoy yourself. Looks to me that you have spent a good long time with nothing more exciting in your life than counting out your money.'

Colonel Farrance laughed out loud at that. 'Yes, that is one way to put the case. Maybe I shall be interested to see if I am still able to handle myself in something of this nature. It has been a long time.'

His daughter normally burst into any room unbidden, but now that they had a visitor staying in the house, she was a little more circumspect about this. This morning, when she knocked on the door of the library, she waited until her father asked her to enter.

'I learned a lovely tune today. I wondered if you and Mr Wilson would like to hear me play it?'

Ikey Wilson said at once, 'Speaking for myself, Miss Charlotte, it would be a pure pleasure to hear you play.'

The girl reddened slightly at this and then, when her father had nodded approvingly, she put the violin to her chin and played a melancholy air from an Italian opera. Wilson listened, apparently captivated by the music. When she had finished the piece, he said to Charlotte, 'That was real nice. I used to play a little myself on the fiddle, but nothing to match that.'

'Oh, do you play the violin as well?' asked the girl. 'Do play something.' She handed him the instrument and he looked at it long and hard. The feel of the thing in his hands evidently evoked old memories. Then he raised it to his chin and played a merry jig.

'Why, Mr Wilson,' said Farrance's daughter, 'you are quite a musician!'

'Nothing of the sort,' he replied. 'I used to play for fun back a few years.'

'All right, Charlotte,' said her father. 'That will do for now. Mr Wilson and I have business to attend to.'

After she had left the room, Wilson said, 'You are a lucky man, Bob. I never had any sort of family to speak of. I see what I have missed.'

'It's not too late for you to think on that. When once we have righted things and obtained your share of what Crawley has. There is nothing to hinder you from settling down in a little place and maybe taking a wife. You cannot yet be fifty.'

'Forty-eight,' said Wilson. 'Yes, it would be nice to think that something of the kind might come to pass.'

After they had eaten at midday, Farrance suggested that it might be a smart move to try out the guns that he had purchased and familiarize themselves with the handling of them. 'It is some years since I even touched, never mind fired, a pistol. I am apt to be awful rusty.'

Wilson shot him an amused glance. 'I will take leave to doubt that. You were the deadest shot of us all and there were some pretty good marksmen in our band, as you yourself know. Not to mention where I guess you was in the army after that. No, I make no doubt but that you will be able to shoot as well as ever you could.'

Colonel Farrance did not wish to attract overmuch attention to the fact that he was going to practise some shooting and so he left the rifles behind at the house and they took only the two Remingtons into the hills with a box of fifty cartridges. These were carried not in holsters, but hidden away in a saddle-bag. To anybody watching, it would have looked like the two middle-aged men were going only for a sedate ride in the countryside.

When they were what Farrance judged a suitable distance from his home, they stopped in a little valley, where they were unlikely to be over-looked or observed. Neither man had handled a pistol for some years and so they had to experiment a little to see how to open the chambers and insert the shells. Both were more used to muzzle-loading pieces, which needed to be charged from a flask of powder, than they were to guns like this, which used fiddly little brass cartridges.

'I like the feel of this long barrel,' said Ikey Wilson. 'It gives the right balance. Puts me in mind of the old Navy Colt.'

'Yes, the balance is right,' said Farrance. 'I don't care for this lanyard ring, though. I would say that it is a racing certainty that that will get caught up in something and you will fumble the draw.'

'I guess we can remove them, though,' said Wilson. 'They are a sight easier to load than a cap and ball, that's for sure.'

About twenty-five yards from them stood an old pine tree. Farrance took the pistol in his hand and then looked at the tree, gauging it to be an enemy. Then he raised the gun, cocking it with his thumb as he did so, and fired without hesitating. He drilled the tree at once, about six feet from the ground. 'You woulda knocked his hat off,' said Wilson, 'but he would have time to shoot you.'

'It kicks higher than I expected,' said the colonel. 'I am used to .36, like the Navy model. It will take a while to get used to this wider bore.'

It took only another half-dozen shots for Farrance to get the hang of the piece and learn how to compensate for the greater recoil to be expected from a .44 revolver, as opposed to the lighter ones to which he had been used.

Wilson was deadly with the thing from the first shot. He had always had a natural facility with weapons, a skill which had drawn him to Farrance's attention way back in 1859 and had been the chief quality which had recommended the young man to him and given him to suppose that 'Mad Ikey' would make a fitting member of his gang.

They used up the whole box of shells and by the end of that time both felt comfortable with the pistols. Just as Farrance had said, the lanyard ring had an awkward habit of catching on things. This was an army model, which accounted for the inclusion of such an irritating detail.

The two men rode back to Farrance's house at a walk. After they had travelled for a mile or two in companionable silence, Wilson said, 'Have you any ideas on how to tackle this business?

Like you, I hope that we can deal with it without gunplay. All else apart, Crawley lives on a ranch and there are a number of tough young men on the place. If it came to shooting, we might not come off best.'

'I have given the matter some thought,' said Colonel Farrance, 'and what I thought is this. I will send word to him to meet me somewhere neutral and public, like a hotel or some such. Then, when once he arrives, he will see how the case stands and we can talk it over like reasonable men.'

'That sounds fine, as far as it goes,' said Wilson, 'but I do not believe Andrew Crawley to be a reasonable man. I think he will refuse.'

'It depends how the matter is set out before him. I know Crawley.'

'I am mindful that you are helping me with this, although you do not have to. I am grateful.'

Farrance looked surprised. 'You have no occasion to be grateful, Ikey. I let you down badly once, when you had risked your own life to save mine. I would be a dog not to lend you a hand now that the positions are reversed. I am a man who pays his debts, you know that.'

The next five days were occupied with making plans and arrangements. Colonel Farrance had various business interests which he wished to check on before leaving, even though he hoped to be away only a week or two at the most. He proposed that he and Wilson should travel most of the way to the district where Crawley lived by railroad and then hire horses when they were a little closer to their destination.

During these days of preparation, Ikey Wilson had little to do and so took to spending time with Charlotte Farrance. At first, the colonel was a mite uneasy about this, but he soon realized that his anxieties were groundless. There was nothing sinister or carnal in Wilson's attentions to his daughter. It was no more than a man who had been deprived of all female company for over a decade, finding that it was pleasant to listen to the conversation of a young woman. For her part, Charlotte made something of a pet of the older man, playing her violin for him and displaying the drawings and watercolours that she had produced.

At last, it was time to leave. The precise relationship between the colonel and the ragged stranger remained obscure to everybody in the house and Farrance wanted it to remain that way. The rifles and pistols were packed into a trunk, along with the rough clothes that he would be wearing once they were a little nearer to Crawley's home. There were two purposes in planning to dress in a lower style than that to which he was used. In the first instance, there might be some sleeping-out involved and he hardly felt inclined to ruin his good clothes by sleeping on the ground in them. Secondly, he did not want Crawley to gain the impression that he was too well off. Otherwise, he would probably think that he, Farrance, could provide any money that was needed to Ikey Wilson. No, he was as determined as Wilson himself to see that Crawley paid what he owed.

'Do you have gun belts or holsters?' asked Wilson, the day before they left.

'Yes, I have put them in the trunk with the other stuff. I don't know what the fashion runs to in such things these days. I dare say that we shall look like old fossils no matter what.'

'It is not as common now to see men wearing guns in public,' said Wilson sadly. 'When I was young, a fellow did not feel dressed unless he was carrying a gun. Times change.'

'I have observed the same thing,' said Colonel Farrance. 'Which is to say that not all men carry weapons now, the way as was once the case. Folk are more apt to settle their differences in the courthouse than they are to fight the matter out man to man.'

'Well,' said Wilson ruefully, 'I should not think that I could go to law to claim back from Crawley money that we got by robbing a train.’

‘No, that is true. Howsoever the world changes, there will always be times like this when it comes down to men sorting things out by their own efforts.’

3

Ikey Wilson had been reluctant to reveal the exact whereabouts of Andrew Crawley to the colonel. His coyness on the subject was explained when he was finally prevailed upon to deliver the information. This was when Farrance was making arrangements to book the trains.

'Crawley's ranch is up on the Arkansas River,' said Wilson, at last, 'right by the line between Kansas and Colorado.'

'You mean,' said Farrance, 'not far from Evansville, where I was nearly hanged?'

'Yes, that is so.'

'You kept that quiet,' said Farrance, none too pleased.

'I was afraid,' admitted Wilson with disarming candour, 'that had you known right away where I wanted you to go with me, it might have put you off.'

'Well,' said Colonel Farrance. 'It changes nothing. I said I would give you my aid and so I will. Are there any other such little surprises that you have kept hidden from me? If so, then now is the time to bring them forth.'

But it appeared that this was the only material circumstance that Ikey Wilson had thought it prudent to conceal. Other than that, the whole thing was a true bill as he had presented it.

Three trains would be necessary to get the two men to where they were going. First, a local train to take them to where they could connect up with the line to Chicago and then the Atchison, Topeka and Santa Fe railroad, heading west. This would, after a considerable distance, run along the north bank of the Arkansas, before veering south to Albuquerque. Farrance ordered his carriage to be ready to take them to the railroad station, which was some seven or eight miles distant from his home.

The journey was gruelling, despite the fact that Colonel Farrance had enough money to furnish them with every luxury. Ikey Wilson was constantly amazed at all the changes that were apparent since he had been out of gaol. His travelling before had been by back roads and byways, where things were pretty much as they had been since before the war. But the cities! He was dazzled by everything he encountered and was constantly asking Farrance about new developments. 'They say that there is now a talking telegraph, such as will carry your voice, as natural as if you was in the next room. Is this true?' he asked.

'Why, yes,' said Farrance. 'You mean the telephone. I have used one in Pittsburgh. It is a remarkable and uncanny thing to find yourself talking to a fellow hundreds of miles away.'

'Sounds like table-turning or spiritualism.'

'Yes, it can be eerie.'

They alighted, after several days, at Garden City in Kansas. Now although this was right near to where he had been held in gaol all those years back, Colonel Farrance was not really uneasy in his mind about the past. It would need bearing in mind when dealing with Crawley, because he too had taken part in the raid on the gaolhouse that March day just before the war began. This very fact, though, would make him less likely to start stirring up old memories of those long-past days. By Ikey's account, Crawley himself was nicely set up now and would not want to jeopardize his life for the sake of revenge.

Revenge! Had Wilson but known it, he could not have made a better appeal to the colonel than by invoking the name of Andrew Crawley. Every day, Farrance was reminded of that bastard and what he had done. He might well have offered to help Ikey anyway; Crawley's involvement in the matter made it a racing certainty.

They stayed a couple of nights in Garden City, just long enough to hire horses and buy provisions. Farrance rented a hotel room and desired the proprietor to keep it with their things within for as long as necessary, making a down payment to cover the next seven nights. The owner of the hotel looked at him as though he had taken leave of his senses, but it was nothing to him if a man was crazy enough to pay to keep a room empty.

After breakfast, Farrance changed into the working man's clothes that he had brought with him. Wilson was already dressed so, causing the staff at the hotel to assume him to be some employee of the other man. When they were both dressed in the same nondescript fashion, the colonel took the firearms and ammunition from the trunk. They had already removed the lanyard rings from the two pistols and now they loaded them. Force of habit caused both Wilson and Farrance to leave an empty chamber under the hammer, although with the machined, centre-fire cartridges that such pistols as these fired, this precaution was not strictly necessary.

The gun belts that the colonel had brought with them had definitely seen better days, but were serviceable enough for their purpose. The two men practised drawing a few times. These were most decidedly not quick-draw rigs, but they would do. After buckling on their pistols and placing Stetsons on their heads, they were ready to leave. They picked up the rifles and left the room, proposing to walk down to the livery stable.

It was strange to walk along the street with a pistol slapping at his thigh. Strange, but not altogether unpleasant for Farrance. He had not seen it necessary to confide in Ikey Wilson, but the truth was that he was not at all displeased to find himself on a little jaunt of this nature. Life at home was fine enough, but mighty dull at times. This episode had jolted him out of his familiar groove and catapulted him back into a world he hardly remembered. It was good to be doing something *useful* for a change. His household and also the businesses in which he had a stake all ran smooth as clockwork without any interference from him. He knew that in his absence, the house would continue to operate efficiently and that this would be so, whether or not he was present.

The game that he was up to now with 'Mad Ikey' was a bird of a different colour. There was not a living soul to help Wilson and if not for him, then nothing would happen to advance the man's prospects. He, Robert Farrance, was indispensable and that was a feeling that he had not had in a good, long while.

Colonel Farrance had specified that he and his friend wanted tough, hardy ponies that would be up to a few days' rough riding across country. He did not want some elegant thoroughbred that looked good trotting up and down the street but would be no use for hard work. The fellow at the stable assured him that both the mounts that he was providing would go all day without a break. 'They're Indian ponies,' he said. 'Bought them from a man who trades with the redskins. Lovely little beasts. You mind you bring them back again safe and sound.'

Once they were clear of the town and on the road, Wilson and Farrance fell to talking over old times. They shot the breeze in this way for a space, both enjoying the sensation of being foot-loose and fancy free. It was in this relaxed and carefree frame of mind that they ran smack bang into trouble without the slightest apprehension of its approach.

Now it was nowhere near as common as it had been even a few years earlier, but there were still young men who made a living out of waylaying travellers and relieving them of their horses, money and anything else that they might have about their person which was worth stealing. Some called these types 'road agents'; they were very much like the highwaymen of old who once infested the lonely roads of England. There were fewer and fewer such men in the United States each year as communications improved and law and order came to even the remotest corners of the land. Still, at that time there were some lazy and vicious men who found it more convenient to prey on their fellow men and women than they did to get a job and work for their money.

The first intimation of anything amiss came when Colonel Farrance and his companion rounded a bend to find three young men on horseback loitering in the road ahead. As they hove into view, the three men fanned out and blocked the way. One of them, who Farrance took to be the leader, was cradling a sawn-off scattergun in his arms, which was pointing in their general direction. This young man, who could scarcely have been more than twenty, cried out when he saw them, 'Hold up, old-timers, we have need to talk to you.'

'What's the case?' asked the colonel.

'It is this. I want you and your friend to advance at a walk. And do not make any move for your guns, neither.'

Both Farrance and Wilson had seen what fearful injuries could be inflicted with a scattergun at close range and so made no quick movements such as might be open to misinterpretation by a trigger-happy young gunman. They walked their ponies forward until they were only ten or fifteen feet from the three men. All were young and it struck Farrance that they might not even be twenty years of age. The boy with the scattergun could have been seventeen or eighteen.

'It's like this, old men,' said the leader of the group. 'We have taken a liking to your horses and so on. In short, this is a hold-up.'

'Are you really sure that you want to do this, son?' asked Farrance, in a fatherly voice. 'We are not looking for trouble.'

'Don't you call me 'son',' said the boy. 'I ain't your son, you old bastard.'

'I was only trying to be civil,' said the colonel mildly. 'I do not like to see a fellow your age taking the wrong road.'

'Never you mind what road I am taking, you cowson. Now take out that pistol of yours, real slow. Hand it to me by the hilts.'

'It is not too late. We don't need to do this.'

'That's where you are wrong,' said the boy. 'You surely do need to do this or I will shoot you down.'

The other two young men laughed at this. They clearly thought their leader a real card.

Very slowly, Colonel Farrance reached down and took out the Remington by the trigger guard. Then he allowed it to hang upside down from the trigger guard, with the hilts pointing towards the boy who had the drop on him.

'That's right sensible of you, old man,' said the boy. 'Now walk your horse forward very slowly and hand me that pistol.'

Farrance did as he was bid and edged closer to the young man with the scattergun. Then, when their horses were practically nose to nose, he leaned forward slowly and proffered the gun to the other. The boy was grinning in triumph and allowed his own gun to droop as he reached out with perfect confidence to take the pistol dangling from Colonel Farrance's forefinger.

As the young man's hand was about to close on the hilts of his pistol and just at the very moment when the fellow was assured that he had succeeded in buffaloing this old fool into doing as he was told, Colonel Farrance flicked his wrist upwards sharply, swinging the pistol round the pivot of his forefinger and bringing the hilts into his hand. At that same instant, he cocked the piece with his thumb and fired immediately, hitting the boy in the chest. Then, to make quite sure of the outcome, he fired again; this time into the boy's face. The heavy .44 bullet entered his right eye, before blowing out the back of his head.

Before he had time to turn his attention to the other young men, there came the crash of gunfire from behind him and when he drew down on the others, Farrance discovered that they were already dead. 'Mad Ikey' Wilson had been renowned for his speed and accuracy in contests such as this, twenty years before these boys had even been born.

'The road agent's spin, by God,' said Wilson. 'I never would have thought you were still up to them sort of tricks!'

'Road agent's spin?' said the colonel. 'I seem to recollect that we knew that stunt as the border roll. No matter; it was not something which those boys had seen before.'

It is a fearful thing to snuff out young lives in this way and both Wilson and Farrance were only talking in this bantering way to ward off the sadness at seeing three fellow beings with their lives before them sent in this way to early graves. 'It is the hell of a thing,' opined Colonel Farrance, 'to see three youngsters die so needlessly.'

'Still and all, they did not have to try and rob us. I reckon their blood is upon their own heads.'

'It could be so, Ikey, it could be so.'

They rode on in a more subdued frame of mind than before. After they had travelled in silence for perhaps a quarter-hour, Wilson said, 'You coulda shot me back there and blamed it on them fellows.'

'Shoot you? Why would I do that?'

'Oh, I don't know. You mighta thought that I was a nuisance to you and was likely to tell folks about your past history. Any reason.'

'Ikey, if I was planning to shoot you, it would not be by catching you unawares. I would challenge you first. You forget the rattlesnake code?'

Ikey Wilson laughed out loud. 'Lordy,

Bob, I have not heard that mentioned these many years. Nobody sets mind to such foolishness these days.'

'Well, I do,' said Farrance. 'I lived my life by that code when I was young and I would scorn to go against it now that I am old. You recall that you always gave warning if you were going to attack. Just like a rattlesnake. None of us in those days would have shot a man in the back or killed an unarmed one. It would not have been honourable. Even the worst of villains would have been disgraced to attack a man from behind.'

'Well now,' said Wilson, 'I think times have changed since last we was on the scout. Look at how those Ford brothers served Jesse James a few years back.'

'Yes and look now at how the matter is viewed. Jesse James has become a hero and those Fords are regarded as the dirtiest dogs who ever drew breath.'

It would take another day's riding before they could hope to reach Endeavour, the little town near to which Andrew Crawley had his ranch.

This meant sleeping out in the open for the night; which prospect Colonel Farrance viewed with no little trepidation. As night descended, Wilson said, 'I'll warrant it is some while since you slept out of doors, Bob. Am I right?'

'I do not say that you are wrong, Ikey. Nor can I pretend that it is a prospect which is an attractive one to me. I am past sixty, you will recall.'

'Hell, I am nearly fifty myself. I have been sleeping in God's open air ever since I come out of gaol. It has done me no harm.'

'Judging by the state of you when you fetched up at my place, it had not done you a power of good either,' remarked Farrance.

They chose a small gully to camp in for the night. Farrance had brought sufficient food for a decent meal, which they ate by the light of the fire they had lit. There was even a half-bottle of brandy to share. When they had eaten their fill, the two men lay back in contentment. Ikey Wilson said, 'How does it feel to be on the rampage again? After living as a respectable citizen for all those years, does it not feel a mite strange?'

The colonel thought about this question and then said, 'It does and it doesn't, Ikey. I have never entirely been able to take myself seriously as an honest and upstanding member of the community, if you take my meaning. It has always seemed like I am playing a role, like it may be that I am in a play or something. It is at times like today that I come to be who I really am.'

The other man sat up and looked sharply at his old comrade. 'That is the hell of a thing to say, Bob. You mean that you wished that you were not well off and able to live a peaceful and enjoyable life?'

'No, not that exactly. But when you have good food on the table every day and as much of it as you want, when you don't need to long for something because you have the wherewithal to buy it at once, when every day is safe and there is no danger worse than having to pay more taxes . . . Under such conditions, life can become a little dull. It is no more than that.'

'There is worse things in life than it being dull, I can tell you that for certain sure.'

'Yes,' said Farrance. 'I make no doubt of it. But food without salt and pepper can become a little wearisome.'

There was silence for a spell and then Wilson said, 'Do you remember that time we knocked over that stage in Texas? Is that the sort of spice you are longing for in your food?'

The colonel chuckled quietly. 'I had not called that to mind these many years. That was the day that Jack Larsen was killed. That was the hell of a thing.'

'You might say so. I have a picture in my mind of that day, which came when you was complaining about your life lacking seasoning and spice. There were four of us. You, me, Jack Larsen and Andrew Crawley. I do not rightly mind where the rest of the boys were at that time, nor why the four of us alone engaged to take that stagecoach.'

Farrance sat up and stared into the darkness. 'Did we not hear some story or rumour about there being gold on board? I mind that gold was mentioned by somebody.'

'It could be so,' said Wilson. 'Anyways, we stopped that coach and all four of us had handkerchiefs tied round our faces. We must have looked a regular crew of desperate villains. You remember how that fellow riding shotgun just threw down his weapon at once and put up his hands? I can still see the disgusted look on the driver's face that the man whose job it was to protect the stage had surrendered so quick and easy.'

'Yes, I remember that well. We had not thought that it would all go so pleasant and agreeable. Then, just as we were getting ready to shake down the passengers and rifle the luggage, that old fellow leaned out of the window to see what was going on and what the delay was.'

'Yes, and a second later, he had drawn a gun and just shot Jack dead on the spot.'

'I never was so surprised in the whole course of my life,' said Colonel Farrance thoughtfully. 'Who would have thought such a thing would happen? Larsen just fell off his horse and you and me shot back at the old man and then the driver went for his gun in all the confusion.'

Wilson said, 'Yeah, but he did not draw it, because we shot him. The horses went mad and that stage went careering off down the road, took a bend at speed and overturned.'

Farrance shook his head sadly. 'One way and another, we ended up killing or maiming all except one person that was on that stagecoach. What did we have to show for it, Ikey? There was no gold and I doubt we got more than fifty dollars in cash money.'

'Well,' said Wilson, 'that's right. You

were talking about your life now being a lack of excitement or zest and I wanted only to remind you how it really was with us then. One minute, we're laughing and joking with Jack Larsen and the next he was dead. I don't know about you, Bob, but I can surely do without 'spice' in my life of that kind.'

After a little more desultory talk, mingled with reminiscences of this sort, Farrance and Wilson settled down to sleep. Ikey Wilson drifted off almost at once, but Farrance could not get comfortable on the ground. Everywhere he lay seemed to him to have a peculiarly sharp stone positioned right beneath a sensitive portion of his anatomy. Then, just as he had got himself into a good spot and was almost asleep, the urge came upon him to empty his bladder. He had been having difficulties in this department for the last year or two, but it did not really signify in his home, where there was a chamber pot ready to hand beneath his bed. Here, he had to get up and walk off a space to make water.

The chilly night air made matters worse and after going through this performance three or four times, he succeeded in rousing Wilson from his slumbers, who asked, 'What ails you, Bob? Problems with your waterworks?'

'Something of the kind,' replied Farrance, a little embarrassed. Eventually, he was able to fall asleep, only to waken at the first flush of dawn, his bladder feeling once more uncomfortably full.

4

The little town of Endeavour nestled in the lee of a range of hills, right on the border between Kansas and Colorado. So close was it to the line between the territories, that at different times both Kansas and Colorado had claimed jurisdiction over its inhabitants.

Andrew Crawley had, according to Wilson, a vast, sprawling ranch to the north of Endeavour, on which he bred horses. It was not clear how he managed to maintain such a prosperous lifestyle through this activity alone; but there it was. He was a rich man and held of great account in the town.

Endeavour was typical of many small towns in that part of the country. The earliest citizens had built and lived in rough soddies, many of which were little better than mud huts. Later, these had been supplemented by wooden buildings and so the town had grown, until it now boasted many of the features of a civilized community: stores, church, saloon, livery stable, brothel and so on. It was, at this time, home to perhaps five or six hundred souls.

Before entering the town, Farrance and Wilson paused on the road. The colonel had a few words that he wished to deliver to his companion and it was his conviction that this had best be done forcibly and while the two of them were alone.

'I wish to make something very plain,' said Farrance. 'Without chasing round the woodpile, it is this. I engage to help you get your just deserts from Andrew Crawley, who, as we both well know, is a damned villain. I have not come here to be party to any act of bloody vengeance, though. I have kitted us out like this so that if it comes down to it, we may fight or defend ourselves. I do not look for a violent outcome.'

Wilson looked at him oddly. 'I might

have said the same to you, Bob. You told me to mind my own affairs on that score, but I think you have as much reason as I have to exact revenge upon Crawley.'

'Tell me now, did he tell you what was between us?'

'That he didn't. Only that the last time he saw you, you were in pursuit of him and he feared for his life.'

Colonel Farrance said nothing more and the two of them walked their ponies down the slope into Endeavour.

Small though it might have been, Endeavour was a cheerful, bustling town. The main street looked neat and tidy and there were more smiles than frowns to be seen on those passing to and fro. The first thing to do was find a place to rest their heads for the day or two that Farrance hoped would be all the time needful to clear up this misunderstanding. He put it in those terms when thinking of it — as a 'misunderstanding'. It somehow made the business sound less threatening and not so likely to end in bloodshed. Misunderstandings could always be cleared up without too much fuss and bother, which was just what he hoped to do here.

The Busted Flush saloon had rooms to rent by the night, one of which was furnished with two single beds. This sounded the very thing. As he and Wilson washed some of the trail-dirt away, Farrance said, 'What do you think would be the best dodge for contacting Crawley? I do not favour the idea of riding out and interviewing him on his own territory. I think that it would be better to meet here in town. All else apart, that might give less opportunity for treachery and suchlike. He would be constrained by the fact that there were many witnesses to his actions.'

'When I was here a couple of months back, there were always men of his drinking in this here saloon. I should think that you might get one of them to carry a message to his boss.'

'When do they come here?' asked

Farrance. 'Mostly in the evening?'

'Yeah, I reckon.'

'I suppose that there would be no harm in asking around a bit and seeing what people have to say about Crawley. What is his outfit called?'

'The Double Star.'

The barkeep did not appear to be overly enthusiastic about cooking up a meal just for a couple of travel-stained saddle bums. He offered, however, to provide them with bread and cheese, if that would suit. It looked as though it would have to. When he brought them some buttered slices of bread with a hunk of cheese to go with it, Farrance asked, 'I hear there's a fellow called Crawley in these parts. Would you happen to know anything of him?'

'Mr Crawley has a big ranch. He is very well respected around here.' Colonel Farrance noticed the slight but unmistakable emphasis upon the word 'Mr'. By 'well respected' he took it that Crawley and his boys spent a deal of money in the town. He said, 'I am minded to send a note to Mr Crawley. Do you know if any of his men are likely to be in town this day?'

'His boys are always around,' said the barkeep. 'I will point out some to you later, if you are here.'

'Thank you, that is right nice of you.'

When he went back to the table where Wilson was sitting, the colonel said, 'I don't see that we shall have any difficulty contacting Crawley. I suppose that you will be wanting a beer or some such?'

'Whiskey would be better.'

Later that day, Farrance reproached himself for not sticking firm at this point. But as he was about to make some remark upon the wisdom of supping ardent spirits before noon, he thought that here was a man who had been caged up in a penitentiary for better than ten years. Why should he not be allowed to indulge himself a little? He went to the bar and ordered a bottle of whiskey.

'What was it like in gaol?' he asked

and then as soon as the words were out of his mouth realized what a damned stupid question it was. Wilson did not look to mind, though. He shrugged.

'When you are locked up, there is no point thinking about being free. You would go clean out of your mind were you to dwell upon all the things you was missing through being in a cell. I got by as best I could.'

They talked of this and that for a while and Farrance noticed that the level in the whiskey bottle was sinking with alarming rapidity. He himself had only poured a small measure, most of which remained undrunk. Wilson, on the other hand, was knocking the stuff back like it was soda pop.

It was while he was trying to decide what, if anything, he should do about Wilson's evident determination to become intoxicated, that Farrance saw the barkeep pointing in their direction and speaking to a tough-looking individual who was staring towards them with a suspicious look upon his face. This man came over to their table and stood gazing down at them. Wilson, who had been growing gloomier and gloomier, had been staring at the floor moodily, but looked up when the fellow came nigh to where they were sitting. Their eyes met and they recognized each other at once. A slow and contemptuous smile spread across the face of the standing man.

'Say,' he said, 'I know you. I beat up on you and slung you off the Double Star a while back. I thought you would have got the message. What are you doing back round here now?'

'You beat up on me?' asked Wilson in a dangerous voice. 'You mean you was one of six who beat me. You durst not tackle me alone, you have not the balls for it.'

'Shut up, Ikey,' said Colonel Farrance. 'We are not looking to start any fighting. Recollect what I told you.' Addressing the man who was looming over them, Farrance said, 'Would you care to join us for a drink? I have it in mind to speak to your boss.'

'What for?'

'That's my affair. If I write him a note, will you deliver it to him? You do work for Crawley?'

He thought that he had smoothed things over very neatly and averted what had threatened to be a nasty situation, when Ikey Wilson lurched to his feet and said to the cowboy, 'Your mother was a dirty, pox-ridden whore and as for your father, he mighta been any one of a hundred men.'

The man's face went first white and then dark red. He said in a strangled voice to Wilson, 'Not in here, you mouthy bastard. Let us go out back and see if you will sing the same tune.'

Realizing that it was hopeless to try and prevent a fight now, Farrance said, 'There will be no gunplay, only fists. I will come and set a watch to make sure that the fighting is fair.'

The cowboy sized up Farrance and said, 'You want to mix yourself up in this here, then good luck to you. Don't blame me if you end up with a whipping as well as your friend.'

'I don't look for that to happen,' said the colonel. Then he said to Wilson, 'This is just precisely the thing which I hoped to avoid. Will you not make your peace with this fellow?'

'After I rub his face in some horse shit, I might consider it,' was the uncompromising reply.

Behind the saloon was an undeveloped parcel of land upon which folk in the town had an unfortunate tendency to dump any items for which they had no further use, ranging from broken chairs to bits of rusty metal. They were very strict about fighting in the Busted Flush and those wishing to give proof of their pugilistic prowess were obliged to leave the premises and come round to the back here.

As they headed round the side of the saloon, Farrance said to Ikey in a low voice, 'You damned fool! What did you want to start this for?'

'Because that bastard could not tackle me alone and called for his friends to join in. He could not best me when it was just the two of us and I want now to show him his error.'

'You are casting everything into hazard. I suppose you know that?'

'Not a bit of it,' said Wilson. 'We can still send a message to Crawley by somebody else. This is not queering our pitch in the least.'

A number of loafers had trailed round with them to see the fun. Cartwright, the man from the Double Star who Wilson had fronted, was renowned locally as a cunning and dirty fighter. The man was a bully and braggart and most of those who had come to watch would have been only too pleased to see this oaf come to grief.

Colonel Farrance tried one last time to stop the fight. He said loudly to both Wilson and Cartwright, 'You have both showed that you are not afraid to fight. What say that we all just shake hands now and go back inside, where I will buy drinks all round?' Neither man took any notice of this speech, both staring with hatred at the other. When Farrance could see that there was no way round it, he said, 'Well, if fight you must, then let's have your guns over here with me. Let it be a fair fist fight with no biting, gouging, scratching or similar underhand tricks.'

As the two men removed their shirts, it struck Farrance that Ikey Wilson was not half as drunk as he had made himself out to be, despite sinking over half a bottle of whiskey.

Wilson and Cartwright had barely faced each other before Cartwright swung a fist like a hock of ham at the other man's head. Wilson jumped back and landed a hard kick to Cartwright's shin, causing the other man to grunt with pain and move back out of reach. Colonel Farrance had pronounced the traditional formula about having a clean fight, but had had no real expectation that either of the contestants would refrain from unsavoury practices when once they had got into the swing of the thing.

Cartwright was much bigger than Ikey Wilson. He was a great bear of a man, but it crossed the colonel's mind that his old companion was the more dangerous of the two. Watching Wilson now and noting the look on his face, Farrance began to worry that his intention had not all along been to commit murder under the guise of a fight. He tried to recall if he had seen a knife or anything of that nature among Ikey's belongings.

Cartwright was watching his adversary warily. Then he made a rush at Wilson and tried to hug the smaller man to him, presumably with the aim of using his greater size and strength to crush the smaller man's ribs. Ikey Wilson let Cartwright get right close and then bent down swiftly and struck the other man with a careless, but extremely hard, blow to the groin. Then he darted back again, out of reach. Cartwright doubled up in agony, whereupon Wilson ran back and delivered a few well-aimed kicks to his opponent's head and neck, causing him to keel over like an old oak tree which had been felled. Once Cartwright was lying prone, Wilson moved in for the kill, but Colonel Farrance had seen about enough. He called out, 'Ikey, that's the limit. You will kill him and where's your advantage then?'

Wilson stopped dead in his tracks and the words worked on him to some purpose, because instead of attacking the fallen man, he instead undid his pants. Then he urinated on the head of his vanquished foe, to the delight of the watching crowd.

'You mad fool,' said Farrance, as they went back inside the Busted Flush. 'I made sure that you would kill him.'

'That was certainly what I purposed,' said the other candidly, 'but when you spoke, I saw that it would not help.'

The barkeep called them over and

said, 'There is two more of the Double Star boys over yonder. I dare say you know your own business best, but I would not myself care to get crosswise to Andrew Crawley and his outfit. But it's nothing to me.'

Farrance and Wilson went over to the two men who had been pointed out to them. The colonel said, 'I have a message that I want to reach your boss this day. Can either of you help with that?'

'What's it about?' asked one of the men.

'Crawley won't thank you to meddle in his private affairs,' said Farrance. 'See here, now, I have already written out what I wish to say to him. I desire him to meet me here this evening.'

'That won't answer,' said the other of the two men. 'Mr Crawley does not like saloons. He will not come here; I can tell you that for nothing.'

'He will come. Tell him that 'Long Bob' Farrance sent him this letter. I am sure that he will find time to meet me.'

'Long Bob? What the hell kind of name is that?'

'Never you mind about that,' said Farrance. 'Just you deliver this to your boss. You men are not going to be drinking here all day, I suppose?'

'It's nothing to you if we are. But no, since you ask, we're heading back to the Double Star in a while. We will give your letter to the boss, but don't look to see him coming here tonight.'

Farrance desired Ikey to go for a stroll with him up and down the street a little, partly to sober him up, but also to talk about how they would play it when Crawley came by the saloon that night. For whatever his men might think, Colonel Farrance knew full well that Crawley would be unable to resist seeing him. He only hoped that he would be able to master his own temper and not surrender to his natural impulses and shoot Crawley down like the mangy dog that he was.

'I want you to keep out of the way while me and Andrew talk things over,'

Farrance said. 'I have the measure of him and know how to set the case before him.'

'Andrew, is it? You and he are suddenly friends?'

'No, he is not my friend, not by a long sight, but we have more chance of getting what we want from him if we keep it agreeable. I do not like him one bit more than you. I tell you straight, I came here to repay a debt to you; I would not have come on my own account.'

They had reached the edge of town and stood looking out to the distant hills. Wilson said, 'You are right about me keeping out of his way. You will be able to bargain better with him. Besides which, after the scurvy way he served me, I might be sorely tempted to put a bullet through his head and that would not help matters.'

'Not hardly. Something else we have not talked of is the exact amount that you would have from Crawley. What quantity of gold did you have as your share from that robbery?'

'We calculated that we had about two stones' weight of gold each, which is to say about twenty-eight pounds.'

Farrance nearly choked at this amazing intelligence. 'God almighty, Ikey, you stand there and tell me that you were possessed of, let me see now . . . ' He tried to work out what twenty-eight pounds multiplied by sixteen ounces to the pound came to but was unable to figure it in his head.

Wilson could see the cogs turning in the colonel's mind as he attempted to cipher the amount that twenty-eight pounds in weight of gold would come to in cash money. Wilson said, 'Twenty-eight times sixteen is four hundred and forty-eight. The price back then was twenty-five dollars an ounce, give or take a little. It comes to eleven thousand and two hundred dollars. I have had eleven years to check and re-check the amount. I did little else while I was banged up in the penitentiary.'

'I see why you are a mite ticked off with the fellow. I guess we might be stuck here for a time, because I do not see how even the wealthiest rancher is going to be able to lay his hands upon over eleven thousand dollars, just like that. I am not a poor man, but it is more than I could do, I will tell you straight.'

Colonel Farrance and Ikey Wilson had been in each other's company pretty much without a break since leaving Pennsylvania and both felt in need of a break from the other. It was agreed that they would go their own ways that day until eight or so, when Farrance had asked Andrew Crawley to attend upon him at the Busted Flush.

It was something of a relief to be free of Wilson, thought Colonel Farrance, as he strolled around Endeavour. He had of late found enjoyment only in his daughter's company and being stuck with another man in this way for days on end was not really what he cared for these days. He had had his fill of that both during his time as an outlaw and also in the army. He would not be sorry when this expedition was over and done with and he could get back to his mundane life. It had been a novelty, walking round like this with a gun at his hip, but a night spent sleeping on the bare earth had done his constitution no good at all and he had tired of this little vacation.

Farrance wondered what had become of the man that Wilson had so comprehensively defeated. He could have wished that Ikey had spared the fellow that final indignity of pissing over him in that way. This was not an insult that any man would be likely to forget in a hurry and he had an idea that Cartwright was not a forgiving sort. It was to be hoped that Ikey Wilson would not do anything else to jeopardize their enterprise. Not for nothing had he been known all those years ago as 'Mad Ikey'. He was generally regarded as a man who would do or say anything at all that he wanted.

The problem was that a fearless fellow who gave not a second's consideration to the consequences of his actions might be an asset for an outlaw gang; he was not, however, much of a help when one was trying to persuade a man gently that he must give up and surrender a large part of his wealth. This was a ticklish job and Ikey's methods had already been found wanting when first he had gone to Crawley with his request.

5

After a long, brisk walk into the hills and back, Colonel Farrance felt sufficiently braced and healthy that he thought he might be able to tackle anything that the rest of the day threw at him. As he walked back into Endeavour, he fervently hoped that Ikey Wilson had managed to keep out of mischief and was not already at the centre of a storm. He needn't have worried, though, because when he went back to the room over the saloon, it was to find Wilson sleeping soundly, the whiskey that he had guzzled down earlier seemingly having acted as a soporific.

'Hey, you lazy fellow,' said Farrance. 'Wake up now. We need to talk.'

Watching Wilson come to and ready himself for action was a startling experience, for there were none of the preliminaries that one saw with most folk when once they had been roused from a deep sleep. Ikey Wilson simply opened his eyes, sat up and swung his legs round to plant his feet on the floor. He looked as bright and alert as though he had just walked into the room and sat down on the bed.

'Lord, Ikey, you are quick off the mark,' said Farrance, after witnessing this. 'It takes me a half-hour after waking up before I am ready to face the world.'

'Happen nobody has cheated you out of eleven thousand dollars,' said Wilson. 'It puts one on edge and eager to get to the task of recovering the money.'

'I dare say that is true. Listen, I want to tell you what I see as the best means of proceeding now. First off is where I wish to speak to Crawley alone. He and I might have some morsel of unfinished business of our own to talk over and I do not want my life's history laid out for the edification of you nor anybody else.' He could see that Ikey Wilson was disposed to argue the point, but held up a hand and said, 'No, Ikey, I will have my way on this. What's done between me and Andrew Crawley is nothing to the purpose here. You want your money back and I will work towards that end. I am not budging on this point.'

Wilson didn't like it, but there was little that he could do about it, so he shrugged and said, 'You will have it your own way, Bob. You were ever so, even back in the old days. You have not changed that much.'

'We have time to eat before Crawley is likely to arrive here. Do not let us fall out over a trifle like this.'

Being nearly evening, there was something more substantial on offer in the way of food when the two men went downstairs to the barroom. It was only meat and potatoes, but they were both ravenously hungry. The fellow behind the bar said, as he took their order, 'I do not look for there to be any fighting here this night. I feel it in my water, you men are bad news. I shall not be sorry when you go and that's a fact.' There was little enough that either Farrance or Wilson could say to this, which was a pretty accurate summation of the case as it stood.

While they ate, Wilson asked, 'What time do you expect Crawley?'

'I said in my note that I would be here in this room from eight of the clock.'

'Do you think that he will come?'

'I make no doubt of it,' said Colonel Farrance. 'No doubt at all, if for no other reason than pure curiosity.'

'Which,' said Wilson, with a sudden and unexpected smile, 'was apt to kill the cat, if I recall the lesson right from my schooldays.'

Throughout the whole of their conversation, although there was not one thing upon which he could lay his hand, Farrance grew more and more certain that Wilson was planning to do something foolish. What it could be, he had no idea at all.

A good half-hour before Crawley was

likely to make his entrance, Ikey Wilson went off for a walk, having first given his oath that he would not show himself nor interfere with the bargaining that Farrance had promised to undertake on his behalf.

The saloon filled up slowly, until by eight it was fairly busy, with perhaps two or three dozen men drinking there. Most tended to congregate at the bar and a number of tables remained unoccupied. Farrance sat alone at a table, nursing a small glass of whiskey. He spotted Andrew Crawley at once when he entered. It had been over fifteen years since he had set eyes upon him, but the man had not changed all that much since then; he still looked reckless, arrogant and overly confident of his ability to best anybody at cards, shooting, lovemaking or anything else.

To save his life, Colonel Farrance could not have brought himself to greet Crawley or even indicate that he had spotted him. In the event, this was not necessary, because Andrew saw his old boss and smiled broadly, making his way across the room like he was coming to welcome a long-lost brother.

When once Crawley was within hailing distance of the table and had commenced to tell the colonel how glad he was to see him, Farrance said curtly, 'You may as well cut out all that crap, Andrew, I am no more pleased to see you than you are to find me in town. Sit down and we will settle this as swiftly as ever we are able to do.'

His smile did not fade in the least as he seated himself at the table and set his drink before him. Crawley said, 'You still have the same way with words, Bob. Short and to the point. I thought that you might have come to talk over old times, but I can see that there is somewhat more on your mind than that.'

'You robbed a train back in 1879, with 'Mad Ikey' Wilson and some few others. He went to prison and you offered to look after his share of the robbery. Now he wants it back again.'

'Well now, you have opened your mouth wide. I wonder if I will be able to fill it. First off is where I would ask what affair this is of yours. Can't Ikey Wilson speak for himself?'

'You know what happened when he came here. Now I am here to aid him and I tell you straight that if you will not deal straight with him, then you had best resign yourself to going up against me. Is that what you will have?'

'Not so hasty,' said Crawley, laughing as though at a hearty joke. 'There need be no talk of you and me going up against each other. Leastways, not yet awhiles.'

Colonel Farrance leaned forward and lowered his voice until it was little more than a whisper which Crawley alone could hear. 'Let us rightly understand each other, Andrew. You don't want to get crosswise to me. I did not come these hundreds of miles to bandy words with you, neither. You owe Ikey Wilson upwards of eleven thousand dollars. If you will not pay up, then by God I will see you lose all that you now have and hold.'

'Well, that is plain speaking, Bob, and I am obliged to you for it. Since you are somehow mixed up in it now, the case is altered. I will not deny that I was hoping not to settle up with Wilson, but now I see things in a new light.'

'You will give him his money?'

'His money? You mean the railroad's money. But yes, I will settle up. You must give me a few days, though, to get it together. Tell me, how is your wife? Anne, wasn't her name?'

At the sound of his dead wife's name on this man's lips, Farrance almost lost possession of himself; which was maybe what Crawley had in mind. Luckily, he recollected himself in time and merely said, 'Don't you set mind to my family, Andrew. Just you think about raising that money before I come calling on you.' He stood up and said, 'I will be in this same place at this time in five days from now. Be very sure that you have the money by then.' He turned and walked away, heading up to the room that he and Ikey had rented.

Ikey was still out and about, so Farrance lay on his bed and considered what had been said by him and Crawley. Was it a true bill? Would Andrew Crawley really do his best to scrape together over eleven thousand dollars and hand it over to Wilson? It was an interesting question. Colonel Farrance set his mind to working out how he would raise such a sum if called upon to do so. He supposed that he could mortgage his house and land at a pinch and probably Crawley could do likewise. It would be placing a burden around his neck, though, especially with interest rates running at current levels. It was more likely by far that the man would seek some convenient method of welching on his debt. He would know by now about the way that Wilson had beaten up that man of his, Cartwright. It would not be easy to arrange for both him and Wilson to be silenced or disposed of while they were in Endeavour. The danger would come if Crawley invited them to go up to the Double Star to collect the money, when once he had supposedly raised it.

Did Crawley know about Charlotte? That was another aspect of the thing which he could not fathom out. Had the man known that Anne was dead? The enquiry after his wife might have been mocking, but still perfectly genuine.

After he had been lying there on the bed for perhaps an hour, turning around in his head every smallest part of the situation, Farrance grew weary of his own company and resolved to go downstairs and mingle with his fellow men for a spell.

The Busted Flush was not a fabulously well-appointed drinking place but the colonel had seen a good deal worse in his time. It was gloomy, but that was perhaps because Farrance was used to gas lighting. The barroom of this saloon did not run to any such luxury, being illuminated only by three enormous kerosene lamps, suspended from the ceiling on pulleys. There were none of the gilt-framed pier glasses that one found in some of the more prosperous establishments either. Nor was there any pianist or faro table. Nothing, except for a bar stretching the length of the room and a dozen round tables scattered about the joint. It was strictly a drinking place, somewhere where men came to escape from their womenfolk and enjoy a glass of whiskey and a smoke.

Farrance worked his way to the bar, easing and wriggling his way gently through the throng. What with the dim light provided by the oil lamps and the fug of smoke, it was hard to see your hand in front of your face in the barroom. Eventually, he reached the bar and ordered his second whiskey of the evening. When it came, he turned round, ready to be sociable and chat to anybody who might be, like him himself, at a loose end. As he swivelled his body round, it was inevitable that he should brush against the man nearest to him. The colonel thought nothing of it, until a voice at his elbow said, 'Mind where you're stepping, you clumsy ape!'

'Were you speaking to me?' asked Colonel Farrance pleasantly. 'I'm sorry if I brushed against you. It is mighty crowded in here tonight.'

The man who had spoken to him did not seem appeased by this fair-spoken apology, saying, 'Am I speaking to you? Well, I don't see any other clumsy apes near to me, do you?'

It was immediately apparent to the colonel that this was a stunt set up by Andrew Crawley as a neat way of sidestepping his obligations. This fellow had been primed to start a fight with him and, it was perhaps hoped, get him out of the cart and off Crawley's back for good and all. It was an old, old trick but none the less effective for that. He said to the man, 'I'll wager that you are employed up at the Double Star.'

'What does that have to do with the

price of sugar?' said the man. 'You knocked into me and spilled my drink all down me.' This was such a palpable lie, that Farrance could not restrain himself from smiling; which action only caused the man in front of him to grow more angry.

'Who the hell are you laughing at?' he said, blustering and raising his voice with the clear intention of making it appear that a quarrel had broken out. 'I do not take kindly to being laughed at, particular not by an old whore's son such as you.'

Colonel Farrance raised his voice, so that it carried above the hubbub of noise in the saloon, and cried, 'I call upon all you fellows to witness what is happening here. I am being pressed into a quarrel that is none of my making. This man is determined to fight with me and it is far from my wish to do so.'

The sound of conversation and laughter slowly died away as everybody present stared at Farrance and the man near him. Anything which happened from here on in would be seen and attested to by dozens of men. There was no chance of any hole-and-corner kind of action where the colonel might come to grief in mysterious and unexplained circumstances.

The bully who had been pushing Farrance and attempting to goad him into some unwise action was taken aback by the course of events and the ingenious way that he had been exposed to public view. He stood for a few seconds, foxed and unable to work out how best to proceed. His instructions had perhaps been to provoke a fight with Farrance and then injure or kill him. Probably, it had been hoped to do this round the back of the saloon and out of sight of many people. Crawley had chosen his instrument badly, because this man did not have the wit to handle the matter with any finesse and had now been manoeuvred into a situation where his actions would be under scrutiny from many witnesses. He decided to make the best of it.

'You folks had better stand clear,' said Crawley's bully. 'Me and this man have to deal with this here and now.'

There was a mad scramble among the patrons of the Busted Flush to get as far from either man as ever could be. The other drinkers were particularly anxious not to be standing anywhere behind either of the two parties, lest they should be struck by stray bullets if gunfire erupted. Nobody wanted to leave the saloon, though. Gunfights were a rare entertainment in these more civilized times and it had been over a year since there had been any shooting of this type.

The barkeep was far from happy about the way events were developing in his saloon and he said, 'Come on, fellows, can you not at least take it out into the street?' Both men ignored him.

A fair duel like this had not been part of the plans as far as Crawley and his man were concerned. In fact Crawley had specifically instructed his hired hand not to brace the colonel in full view of the public, but to wait until they were more or less alone. The fellow was none too intelligent, though, and had difficulty holding more than one idea in his head at a time.

Farrance stood up straight and tall; not for nothing had he once been known as 'Long Bob'. He was far and away the tallest man in the room. The Remington hung at his hip and since Crawley's man was also carrying iron, it looked to the spectators as though this would be a regular duel of the kind that was becoming vanishingly rare as the century drew towards its close.

'Are you sure about this?' asked Farrance, in a calm and collected voice, like he was asking the other man if he wanted to place a large bet on a game of cards.

'Yes,' said the man standing facing him. 'I'm sure.'

The problem was of course that this great, hulking fellow was a dab hand at punching and wrestling; the perfect man to have on your side in a rough house. That was his limit, though, and anything needing brainpower or close reasoning was quite beyond him. He was not especially fast in any respect, even in pulling a gun from its holster. It had never been part of Crawley's plans that it would come to a straight contest between his own man and 'Long Bob' Farrance.

Farrance stood, waiting at his ease and the bigger man in front of him realized that having started this thing, he would be shamed forever in the town if he did not finish it. He grabbed for his pistol, caught his thumb on the belt as his hand snaked down and was still fumbling to get the gun out when Farrance's first bullet took him in the chest. He did not fall down at once, but continued trying to free his gun from the holster, whereupon Colonel Farrance shot him again, this time in the forehead. He turned to the awestruck spectators and said, 'You all saw that this was no wish of mine. His blood is upon his own head.'

The buzz of conversation resumed and people began drifting over to view the corpse, which lay sprawled on the floor in front of the bar. Nobody wanted to get to close to Farrance, either because he had about him the taint of death, or for the more practical reason that he might take it into his head to shoot somebody else. He stood there, a man alone, wondering what to do next. In the end, he figured that he might as well have his drink, which still sat untouched upon the bar.

The owner of the Busted Flush, who also served behind the bar, was none too pleased at this turn of events, coming over to the colonel and saying, 'Didn't I just say that you and your partner would cause trouble here? This is the first killing that has been seen in here for three years. Fine goings-on for a respectable house!'

'I did not start it,' said Farrance quietly. 'You know that fellow was determined to have a fight with me.'

'Whether or not, it is not what I need here.'

'Do you have a sheriff in this town?'

'A sheriff? No, it is peaceful enough in the general run of things. I will have the body moved out back and send word to the Double Star about what happened.'

'Yes,' said the colonel. 'That would be the dodge all right, and you can say that Crawley had best not send anybody else down here to try a similar trick.' He did not wait for a reply, but downed his drink in one gulp, set down the glass and then turned and left the saloon.

It was not quite dark outside; the sky was that beautiful indigo that you sometimes get in summer about an hour after the sun has sunk below the horizon. As he walked slowly along Main Street, he met Ikey Wilson coming from the opposite direction. 'Well,' said Wilson, 'what news?'

'As far as Crawley's debt to you is concerned, he does not deny what you say and engages to settle up with you five days from now.'

Wilson's face lit up with pleasure. 'Does he, by God? That makes for good listening. Anything else? Out with it, Bob, I can tell that that is not the whole story.'

Reluctantly, Farrance told the other of the gun-fight in the saloon and the killing of Crawley's man.

'Strikes me,' said Wilson, after he had heard about this latest episode, 'that you were urging me not to take part in any violent acts and now here you are having killed a man yourself. It is a strange thing.'

'It was planned. Crawley set his bully on me to see if he could get out of paying. I don't think that will be the only game he is up to.'

'Yes, I have already thought on this, before hearing about your little adventure. I have told the owner of that stable where our horses are lodged that we might want the use of his hayloft this night.'

'Did you now?' said the colonel. 'That was right cunning of you, Ikey. Meaning, I suppose, that we might not be safe in that room over the saloon this night?'

'Not safe? Not safe? Our lives won't be worth a wooden nickel if we sleep there tonight. That was already most likely the case, but after you killing that man, it is a racing certainty.'

'I fear that you are right,' said Farrance sadly. 'I was hoping to sleep in a proper bed again tonight. That night out in the open has done my bodily constitution no good, no good at all. I dread the prospect of sleeping on a hay bale. Still and all, there is nothing to be done about it. We had best smuggle our things out of that room without being observed.'

So it was that at the advanced age of sixty-three, Colonel Robert Farrance, late of the Union Army, found himself sleeping rough in a hayloft, as though he were a young boy out on the spree. As for Ikey Wilson, it was nothing to him. The hayloft was a good deal more comfortable than some of the places he had slept since being released from prison and he was quite content with such lodgings for the night.

6

The livery stable was no more than half a mile from the Busted Flush, Endeavour being such a small and compact town. The consequence was that when the shooting began at about two that morning, it was clearly audible from where Farrance lay tossing and turning and sleeping fitfully on the spiky and uncomfortable hay bales.

Colonel Farrance had taken off his gun belt for the night, but laid it close to hand. He found the hilts of the pistol easily enough in the darkness and drew the gun to himself. His rifle was propped up in a corner and he went over and fetched that as well. Then he sat and listened carefully. He was tolerably sure that he had been jerked from his slumbers by a volley of shots and the sound of shouting. He pulled on his boots and then went to the little door which was above the entrance to the hayloft. This gave access to a pulley which was used to hoist sacks and suchlike up into this chamber. The colonel eased open the door a crack and was immediately aware of a ruddy glow over towards the other end of the street, in the same general direction as the saloon.

'Hey,' he said to Wilson, jabbing him urgently in the ribs. 'Wake up. There is mischief afoot.'

Wilson sat up and said, 'What's the case?'

'There's been shooting down the street away and there is a fire as well. I'll take oath it is at the Busted Flush.'

'That sounds about right,' said Wilson. 'But what's it to us? We are safe up here.'

'That won't answer,' said Farrance, at once. 'If there is any gunplay up there, then it is because of us. I could not rest easy unless I was sure that we have not brought anybody else into hazard.'

'Ain't you got a tender conscience?'

grumbled Ikey Wilson, but Farrance could see him pulling on his own boots and buckling on his gun belt. 'What the hell was the point of staying up here, Bob, if as soon as the lightning strikes we go rushing out to place ourselves in harm's way?'

'It won't do. I can't stay here if somebody else is being shot at because of us. You stay here if you will. I am going to investigate.'

In the end, Wilson went with him, as he had known he would.

Just as they had both known it would be all along, the fire proved to be at the saloon. Part of the upper storey was blazing and despite the hour being so early, quite a crowd had gathered to watch. Inside the building, the owner and others were frantically carrying buckets of water up the stairs and throwing them onto the flames. From talking to people watching, it was possible to piece together what had happened, which was this. Some half a dozen men on horseback, all with scarves tied round the lower half of their faces, had broken into the saloon at dead of night and made their way upstairs to the room where until lately Farrance and Wilson had been lodged. They had kicked down the door and poured a perfect fusillade of shots into the room; presumably focusing their fire upon the bolsters which the recent occupants of the room had tricked out to look like sleeping figures.

Either by accident or design, a lamp had been overturned — or perhaps caught by a stray bullet — and the result was that the room had gone up in flames. The saloon was a wooden building, coated with creosote and dry as a tinderbox. Although men were gradually getting the blaze under control, it looked as though a large part of the upper storey had been burnt out. There was no sign of those responsible for this vicious act.

Colonel Farrance took Wilson by the arm and drew him aside from the crowd of onlookers. He said, 'I reckon that we owe our lives to your foresight there, Ikey. Had we been in that room, I believe that we would have been done for.'

'Yes, I'm of the same mind.'

'What do you say to our chances of Crawley paying up in an honourable way after this night's entertainment?'

'Well,' said Wilson, 'I don't see that this alters the case overmuch. I'm not surprised to see him try and wriggle out of his debt in this way by mayhem and murder. That does not mean that when such tricks prove fruitless, he will not pay up.'

* * *

The next morning, after another spell of tossing and turning in the hayloft, Farrance was hobbling about like a cripple. Ikey Wilson, on the other hand, looked as spry and lively as though he had spent the whole night in a feather bed. The two of them breakfasted together at the only eating house in Endeavour. The conversation they heard was all of the shooting and fire-raising the previous night. Meaningful glances were shot at Farrance and Wilson; the story of the shooting in the Busted Flush and the earlier beating and humiliation of Crawley's foreman in the lot behind the saloon now being common currency in the town.

'Where did you disappear to last night?' asked Farrance. 'I mind you were up to something. Was it something as touched upon this present undertaking?'

'You might say so,' replied Wilson. 'I rode out to the Double Star, just to have a little look around. I did not see much of it last time I was there, you know.'

'Why, you damned fool. You will queer the pitch for sure. Were you seen?'

'No, I wasn't seen. I will tell you what, though. Crawley is not making his money from breeding horses. I don't believe that he is running a stud farm or anything like it up there.'

'I will confess,' said Colonel Farrance, 'I was a bit puzzled about that. There is no railroad near here and I don't know who is buying all these horses of his. I thought that there was something odd about that aspect of the thing. What is he up to?'

'I couldn't say. Something criminal, I guess. Beyond that, I could not go. Moonshine liquor? Giving a base to robbers and outlaws? I don't know. I can tell you, though, there are maybe a dozen men up at that Double Star and no more than twenty horses. I only saw a couple of foals. I think he might have a band of his own up there who ride out and get up to different sorts of villainy.'

'The question is, will Crawley be able to lay hands on that eleven thousand dollars? If he is not a legitimate businessman, he will not be able to raise a mortgage on the land or anything like that.'

'It's a damned nuisance. Perhaps I will have to settle for less?'

'Not if I can help it. Having got this far, I mean to see the matter through. You might say that I am like that fellow in the Bible who, having put his hand to the plough, never looks back.'

'What say we ride on up to the Double Star and have a look around? From a distance, that is,' said Wilson. 'We might be able to work out our next step.'

'I do not wish to talk further here. Let's take a turn up the street aways.'

As they strolled along, Colonel Farrance said, 'This puts me greatly in mind of an old proverb. You might have heard it.'

'Which proverb might that be?' asked Ikey Wilson.

'Why, the one as says that 'old sins cast long shadows'. You ever hear that?'

'Heard it,' said Wilson. 'But I do not know that I rightly understand it.'

'It's simplicity itself. You know when the sun is on the point of going down, how long the shadows get? You might have a little bush, no more than five or six feet high, but at sunset, its shadow stretches for hundreds of feet. That's how it is betimes with sins and wrong actions from long back in our past. Their shadows stretch for years and years and touch us when we had forgotten about the deeds themselves long since.'

'You're getting to be a regular poet, Bob,' said Wilson sourly. 'I don't know aught about old sins. It will be enough for me if we can get enough out of Crawley for me to go off and settle down quietly somewhere and live a peaceful life.'

'Yes, I mind that is what we all want when we reach this age, Ikey. Look at me. There I was a few days ago with all my life as quiet and respectable as you could hope for. Then, out of the past comes the shadow of an old sin of mine and before you know it, I'm off on the scout again, like a young buck.'

'All this highfalutin' talk is beyond

me. I am a simple man. Will we go out to the Double Star to take a look?'

'Yes, I suppose that we must. Truth to tell, I am beginning to be of the opinion that Andrew Crawley never had the least intention of handing over any money and has chosen to cross swords with us instead. So be it. It is some good long while since I suffered any man to dictate to me what I could and could not do and I'll be damned if Crawley will be the one to change my habits.'

The Double Star ranch lay an hour or two's ride north of Endeavour as the crow flies. It would have been madness, though, for Colonel Farrance and Ikey Wilson to ride there along the public highway. They might come across an armed party of men from Crawley's outfit and then it could be a tricky and embarrassing encounter. Wilson knew of an Indian path which led up through the hills. For most of this way, they would not be visible at all from the road and it would bring them out overlooking the Double Star at a distance of about a quarter of a mile.

As they walked their ponies along, Wilson said, 'I don't know why you are sticking to me in this, now that the going has got rough, but I want you to know that I am right grateful. When I showed up at your spread, I was ready for you to turn me out at once and that would have been the end of it. You did not need to go to all this trouble.'

'Hell, Ikey, when I say I'll do a thing, then by God I will have it done. You ought to remember that from back when we rode together. I am not one of those lily-livered types who back off when the going gets tough. I said I would help you get your rights from that bastard and I tell you now that I will do it or die in the attempt.'

'Well, it will not be forgot,' said Wilson awkwardly. 'You have played the man and there is no denying it.'

'Crawley is a snake. I knew it even when he was my right-hand man and I never fully trusted him. For the last sixteen years or so, I have had reason of my own for killing him. I would have done too, had I not somebody more important in my life, somebody to care for.'

'You mean your daughter,' said Wilson. 'I tell you now, Bob, I never met a nicer girl since first I drawed breath. She is so kind and friendly and natural. I never could have dreamed that you had it in you to raise a child so, especially a girl child, but she does you credit.'

Farrance was embarrassed at the compliment and sought to hide his emotion by becoming excessively brusque and businesslike. 'We must set out above this ranch of Crawley's for a time, so that I too might get a feel for the place. Not that I doubt you to be right, as touching upon the fact that he is not making his money in the main from breeding horses. I always thought that odd.'

When they were almost in sight of

the Double Star, Farrance and Wilson dismounted and led their ponies to where the buildings and fields of the Double Star lay spread out beneath them like a counterpane. They came over the crest of a hill and then halted, so that they would scarcely be seen from below, unless somebody were looking directly in their direction. Even then, the sun was at their backs and so they were even less apt to be spotted by those on the ranch.

The first thing that Colonel Farrance saw was just the same thing that had struck Wilson: there were hardly enough horses about the place to make sense of this as a prosperous stud farm. It looked rather as though somebody had decided to represent the place in that character and provide a window dressing of horses to maintain the fiction. The colonel said to Wilson, 'If that man is making money from this outfit by buying and selling horses, then I'm a Dutchman. No, you are right, Ikey, there is something else driving this enterprise. Hallo, what's that?'

From a track on the other side of the buildings from where they were standing, a cart was rumbling towards the ranch house and its surrounding buildings. It was not altogether possible to see what the wagon was loaded with, but it did not look to Farrance's practised eye to be anything in the agricultural line. A man came out of the house and directed the driver to take whatever it was on aways to a barn or large shed, about a hundred yards from the main house. The man who had sent the cart in that direction went back into the main house and then reappeared with two other men. The three of them then followed on towards the little barn.

The four men, which is to say the driver of the wagon and the three from the house, then commenced to unload whatever was loaded in the back of the cart. Farrance watched curiously as they picked up large, flat bundles, each about the size of a door, and heaved them, two men to each bundle, into the outbuilding. The parcels, which is what they appeared to be, seeing that they were covered with brown paper and looked as though they were held together with string, were flexible in the middle and sagged distinctly as they were lifted up.

'What do you make to it, Bob?' asked Wilson.

'If I didn't know any better, I would say that they were unloading paper there. Large amounts of the stuff, like they were going to be producing a newspaper or something of that nature. It is a mystery.'

'What had we to do?'

'Why,' said Farrance, 'I wonder you even need to ask, Ikey. We must come prowling along here tonight after dark and see what's what. Are you game?'

'Game?' said Wilson indignantly. 'I was game when you first knew me as a boy and I ain't changed much now that I am well into middle age. Game!'

'Well then, that's what we shall do. I am not sure how we stand with the owner of the Busted Flush. I would suppose that he had guessed by now that it was because of us he had half his house burned down last night. He might not be so ready to offer us another room.'

'Ah, that don't signify. We can stay in the hayloft again. We must offer the man that runs the livery stable a few dollars, but it's nothing to him.'

Once back in Endeavour, the two of them had practically the whole of the day to dispose of and agreed to separate again. It occurred to Farrance that his companion might be in just as much need of solitude as he was himself. After being locked up with other men for eleven years, he was probably gaining pure pleasure from the simple experience of walking about unrestrained by walls and locked doors.

Just as he had suspected, the man at the Busted Flush was not at all keen on seeing either him or Wilson spending another night at his place.

'I find,' said the barkeep, 'that since you and your friend fetched up here, you have shot dead one man in my barroom, your friend beat up another out back and now I am nearly ruined by a fire. You will oblige me by keeping away from my house, you and your friend both.' Which was, reflected Farrance, fair enough, all things considered. You cannot damage a man's livelihood in that fashion and not expect him to be a little ticked off about it.

He did not know which way Wilson had gone in his search for solitude, so the colonel just wandered the town of Endeavour more or less at random, his mind occupied largely with the casual remark he had made to Ikey Wilson about that old saying about old sins and long shadows. Ikey, of course, did not know the half of it. He thought that Farrance was referring to their activities as bandits, back before the war. Well, he was, in a sense, but this dealing with

Crawley had brought the other matter into the forefront of his mind, the thing which had never really left him in the last sixteen and a half years.

On the edge of town, he came to a place where an old log lay fallen. It was as good as a bench in a park and so Colonel Farrance sat himself down upon it and began to brood about the past. In particular, he was casting his mind back to the worst time that he had ever known; far worse than anything which he saw or experienced in the war or even as the leader of a gang of ruthless outlaws. You could put such things out of your thoughts entirely, but the pain of what happened back during those terrible days in 1874 had never left him and sprang unbidden to his mind every time he looked at his beloved daughter. It had begun in March of 1874.

7

Spring came early in 1874. By late March the blossom on the trees was out in Pennsylvania and folk were saying that it was more like May than it was March. Colonel Farrance had not been living in Whyteleafe in those days, nor was he as wealthy as he was later to become. He and Anne had a modest house in Harrisburg, not far from the State Capitol building. He was working his money hard, laying the foundations for his future prosperity. He was well respected in Harrisburg, both as a war hero and a shrewd, but fair, businessman. Life was good. He and Anne had been married for a shade more than two years and were hoping to have a child soon, although there was no real hurry.

Colonel Farrance had married late in life; he was forty-four years of age when he and Anne became husband and wife after a whirlwind courtship. He sometimes wondered if his age had anything to do with the fact that Anne had not yet fallen pregnant, even though they had enjoyed an active and full married life. He supposed that it was just one of those things and there was no hurry. Anne was considerably younger than he was himself. She was not yet twenty-five that March.

He came home from his office that day with no intimation of disaster. A most advantageous deal had been concluded, the one that laid the foundation for his acquisition of the estate in Whyteleafe. There was not a cloud in the sky, not even that little one, no bigger than a man's hand, that scripture warns us to keep a lookout for. The colonel had marched through the front door, called out a cheery greeting to his wife and then walked into the large front room, which overlooked the street. Seated at his ease in that room was Andrew Crawley.

The colonel had not seen Crawley since before the war. When he had abandoned his gang and enlisted, he naturally hoped never again to set eyes upon any of those who had once looked up to him as their leader. Nobody in Harrisburg knew aught of him, other than that he had been an honourable and gallant officer during the war between the states and that he was now a leading figure in the commerce of the town. There was certainly no apprehension that one of their most notable citizens might once have robbed banks and derailed trains for a living. For this reason alone, he was far from overjoyed to come home that day and find Andrew Crawley sitting in his house, being entertained by his pretty young wife.

There was more to the case than this, though. Although Crawley had more or less been his second in command during the outlaw days, he had never cared much for the man. There was something loathsome about him that one was hard pressed to identify. It was just that his presence affected many folk the way that having a venomous snake or poisonous insect near at hand might do. There was an instinctive feeling that here was a man you could never wholly trust. Of course, those qualities were not altogether bad in a ruthless outlaw, but Farrance was strongly repulsed by the sight of this man in his respectable home now. Crawley looked to him grotesquely out of place in a domestic setting.

Anne knew little of his early life, beyond the bald fact that he had been a little disreputable. She certainly could not guess that he had been a murderer several times over when young, nor that he had come within a whisker of having a rope placed about his neck. For this reason, his first thought upon seeing Crawley talking to his wife was how far the man might have opened his mouth.

'Andrew,' he said, with a wide and insincere smile upon his face. 'It surely is good to see you. It must be, how many years now? More than ten, I should say.'

'It was eighteen sixty-one, when last we saw each other, Bob. I mark the day well.'

'Oh,' broke in Anne delightedly. 'Do you call him Bob? I have never known anybody to address him as anything other than Robert or Colonel Farrance. How strange it is to hear him being called Bob!'

''Long Bob' we used to call him back in those days, ma'am. On account of his height, you understand.'

This was dangerous territory indeed. Although his activities had chiefly been confined to Kansas, Colorado and Texas, the name of 'Long Bob' and his gang was pretty widely known at one time. Farrance thought it might be a good thing to find out what Crawley was about and what he was doing here. He said to his wife, 'Darling, I am going to take Mr Crawley into the garden and show him our roses. Not that there are many at this time of year. He used to be a rare one for flowers at one time. Is it not so, Andrew?'

Crawley turned to Anne and said, 'Indeed so, ma'am. And sweet roses ever were my favourites.' He caught her eyes when he said this and stared at her for a second or so, which to his satisfaction caused her to blush slightly. This did not escape Colonel Farrance's remark. He led his erstwhile friend into the garden and then asked as they walked along the path, 'Tell me, Andrew, is my wife observing us from the window?'

Crawley turned to look and then said, 'No, I don't believe that she is.'

Hardly were the words out of his mouth when Farrance had grabbed him around the throat with both hands and dragged him so into a little arbour of rose bushes where they could not be seen from either the house or street. Having got him into this convenient location, Farrance increased his pressure on the man's throat, saying, 'Well, Andrew, you best tell me what your game is, before I choke the life out of you.'

Crawley was no weakling, but he had never been able to stand against Long Bob, especially when one of that fellow's killing rages were upon him. He scrabbled ineffectually, trying to pluck the hands from where they were cutting off the flow of air to his lungs. A second before he began to lose consciousness, Farrance released his grip and gave Crawley an almighty shove, which sent him sprawling to the ground. Then he said, 'Tell me now, what brings you here?'

Crawley could not speak for a time and sat on the earth coughing and spluttering. At length, he said, 'I thought you was going to kill me!'

'Why,' said the colonel, 'that is a mighty strange coincidence, for I thought the same thing myself. I mean it; tell me what you are doing here.'

'I need somewhere to stay for seven nights. Some men are looking for me. They have tracked me this far and I am dead if they catch up with me.'

'What is that to me?'

'You know what it is as well as I do. They catch up with me, then they catch up with you too.'

'So that's the way of it,' said Farrance grimly. 'You would threaten me? I would think you had more sense than that. You know how I have served men before for these tricks.'

'You can't kill me, Bob. Your wife knows we are out here. What will you do, bury my body under your rose trees?'

'Why shouldn't I just pitch you out onto the sidewalk?'

'For one thing, your wife would ask why. For another, I tell you now before God, that if I am taken here, then I will drag you down as well.'

Colonel Farrance came to a sudden decision. 'If you need stay only seven days, then I might see my way to offering you hospitality for that period. But I tell you, try and harm me or my family, then it will go hard with you.

You know me, Andrew. I am a man who does not bluster or bluff. Harm me or mine and there will be a reckoning for it and you had better be ready to pay the price.'

They went back into the house and Farrance said to his wife, 'Poor Andrew here slipped on the path and took a tumble. He is not as sure-footed as he thought himself to be. Have we a cloth or something to wipe the mud from his britches?'

Farrance was not easy about having a cunning reptile like Andrew Crawley in his home, but did not see that he had a deal of choice in the matter. It was, after all, for only for a week.

Until the day that Crawley showed up at his house, Farrance and his wife had lived a life of absolute trust and simple enjoyment of each other's company. There had never been any shadow between them. That changed when Andrew Crawley arrived.

Anne appeared to be pleased and excited at the prospect of having a guest to stay for a week. Ever since he had observed that blush on her cheek when Crawley talked of roses as being his favourite flowers, a slight mistrust had arisen in Colonel Farrance's mind concerning his wife. Andrew Crawley was an insinuating creature and Farrance could not help but wonder if she was charmed by his easy ways. There could be not the least doubt that Crawley went out of his way to pay attention to Anne, not in an obviously seductive way; more as any grateful guest would behaved towards a gracious hostess. Still and all, after three days had passed, Farrance could not rid himself of the terrible fear that his wife would play him false. It might not be a rational anxiety, but it was none the less powerful and disturbing for that.

Farrance could not keep away from the office at this time, much as he would have liked to. Several big deals were reaching fruition and he was negotiating for the estate at Whyteleafe as well. When they were alone after

Crawley had taken his leave and gone to bed, all Anne's conversation seemed to be about him. Practically every sentence she spoke, began, 'Mr Crawley says . . . ' And then, midway through the week, it was 'Andrew says . . . '

Was his wife besotted with the rascal? Or did she perhaps have some schoolgirl crush on him? Or was he imagining the whole thing? Before the week had ended, Colonel Farrance was tormenting himself with the idea that his beautiful young wife was embarking upon an affair with the plausible rogue whom he had himself allowed into the house.

Anne knew that there was something the matter, but Farrance would not let her know the nature of it. He told her merely that his business deals were proving exceedingly vexatious and troublesome and that this was making him a little short with her. And so she spoke more and more with Crawley, who seemed to have nothing better to do with his time than flatter her and, God alone knew if this was true, perhaps flirt also.

Crawley was due to leave the house on the Wednesday. Anne had said openly what a pity it was that he had to go and asked Farrance whether he could not prevail upon his friend to stay any longer, all of which served only to fuel his worst suspicions.

On Tuesday, the day before Crawley was due to go, Farrance was hard at work in his office when it came into his mind that he could go home that very moment and see what was happening in his home. It was reckless of him to take his attention from the business affairs in which he was currently embroiled, but he could not keep his mind on things anyway, even though he had his head buried in ledgers and account books. So it was that at a little before midday on 31 March 1874, Colonel Robert Farrance's life changed for ever and his whole world came tumbling down about his ears.

Everything looked as normal as could

be when he approached the house and Farrance began to think that he was behaving like a damned fool. He opened the front door quietly, not closing it, lest the sound of the catch should signal his presence, and walked noiselessly into the front room. Andrew Crawley and his wife were both there. Crawley had his pants round his ankles and was more or less on top of his wife on the settee. Anne's skirts were all thrown up and she was writhing in what Farrance took to be an agony of pleasure. The second he entered the room, Crawley hitched up his britches and rushed past the colonel and ran straight out of the front door.

He stood there rigid with shock and slowly became aware that Anne was sobbing pitifully. Farrance turned and left the house without a word.

For a week, Farrance stayed in a hotel, sending no word to Anne where he was or what was going on. Then he returned home, to find his wife in a precarious mental state. He moved into the room lately vacated by Andrew Crawley and refused point blank to discuss anything to do with what had taken place. Anne begged and pleaded, but he was utterly immovable. If she started to talk of the matter, he just stood up and left the room. If she pursued him further, he walked out of the house. Despite these strategies, he could not help hearing her say that Crawley had forced himself upon her. He did not know what she meant by this, nor did he care. As far as he was concerned, the marriage was over.

It took a few weeks, but Anne's protestations gradually subsided and she just wandered around the house looking pale and listless. Then one day, a month after Crawley had left, he heard his wife throwing up in the next room. The same thing happened the following day and it dawned on him that she was pregnant.

The fact that he and his wife had not succeeded in having a baby for over two years and then, shortly after he caught her in what he took to be a compromising position, she became pregnant, did not escape the colonel's attention. He could not put the matter into words, not even in his innermost thoughts, but the conviction seized hold of him that his wife was carrying Andrew Crawley's baby.

Somehow, the next eight months passed. What should have been a joyous time that the couple had eagerly looked forward to for years had become a shameful secret. Fortunately, good manners forbade anybody from noticing Anne's condition unless she or her husband acknowledged it, which neither of them did. Farrance drank heavily and stayed late at the office in order to avoid seeing, as much as he could, what he took to be the irrefutable evidence of his having been cuckolded.

One evening, he received word that he should return home at once. He did so, to find that his wife had both given birth to a daughter and died; all in the space of an hour. He was thus left with a child whom he took to be not his own. It was when he was handed this little fragment of mortality that he experienced the closest thing to a religious sensation that he had ever had in his life. He knew that whatever the circumstances which had led up to this helpless child's birth, he alone now was responsible for the welfare and future happiness of this child.

On the midwife's advice, he engaged a wet nurse for the baby, a woman who lived in the poorer part of town. This woman moved in for a time. Not long afterwards, Farrance and the baby moved to Whyteleafe.

At times, the colonel was absolutely sure that the baby was his. There were other occasions when he had no doubt at all that it was not and that he was raising another man's child. It made not the least difference, because as she grew, he came to love the little girl and even when assailed by misgivings, did not think to lay them at the girl's door as some fathers did when there was uncertainty about the parentage of a child.

Farrance loved his daughter Charlotte as though he had no doubts as to who her father truly was. It cannot be denied, though, that from time to time he looked at the child and wondered if he was looking at the natural daughter of the man who had destroyed his peace of mind and wrecked his marriage. He hoped that this never showed by any word or outward sign, but the niggling doubt never left him from the day that the girl was born; was she his child or the product of his cuckoldry?

It might be said that Andrew Crawley had been in some way Colonel Farrance's constant companion over the last sixteen or seventeen years, or at least that his ghost had taken up residence in Farrance's home. He had often wondered what he would do if he set eyes again on the man in the flesh. Had he caught hold of Crawley when he came across that shocking and distressing scene, then murder would probably have been done there and then. However, with the passing years, his passions had faded and died. It was enough for Robert Farrance to know that he and his daughter lived a contented and fulfilled life.

Ikey Wilson's arrival was therefore not in the nature of a wholly unexpected interruption to the peaceful life that Colonel Farrance had been living. He had known all along that there would be a sequel or finishing scene to round off the matter of Charlotte's dubious paternity. He was not best pleased to see Wilson again after all those years, but he would be a liar were he to assert that it was unexpected. He knew that he had unfinished business with Andrew Crawley.

8

Farrance sat on the log, just outside the town of Endeavour, musing over his dealings with Crawley. He stood up and walked back to the eating house where he and Wilson had had their breakfast. He was hungry again and feeling right dispirited and low through dwelling on the past. It was always a bad scheme to think too hard on what was, after all, done and written.

Out of interest, Farrance asked the man who served him up with his food, 'Say, do you know anything about that Double Star place aways north of here?'

'Why you asking?' asked the man curtly. 'You the law?'

'Nothing of the sort,' said Farrance and then on an impulse he admitted, 'I have a crow to pluck with the fellow who runs it, so if he be a friend of yours, then forget I spoke.'

'Crawley, a friend of mine? No, he ain't exactly that. His boys are a mite too fond of throwing their weight around here for me to use that word to describe the fellow.'

This sounded promising and so Colonel Farrance decided to take a step further. 'Fact is, I heard that he might be up to no good on that ranch of his.'

'That's like enough true,' said the man. 'Although what it might be is more than I can say. Nothing in the horse line, though, would be my guess.'

'That is right interesting to hear you say so. Yet others in this town believe it to be so.'

'They do not know what I do, that's the fact.'

'I am listening,' said Farrance. 'And you need not fear me opening my mouth later about anything you tell me, either.'

The colonel and the owner of the eating house were the only people in the place, it being a slack sort of day. 'Well,' said the fellow, 'if you will not blab later about this, then I will tell you. Most people who have business up at the Double Star end up here at one time or another. They deliver goods and come here to eat. Sometimes, people who have popped in there on the off chance to try and sell stuff also come in here and talk. You get the picture?'

'I think so,' said Farrance. 'You mean that you hear odd words spoke about the Double Star.'

'That is about the strength of it. Anyways, one time a fellow who travels in the line of agricultural equipment passed by there and then came into town to eat. He told me that they gave him the bum's rush pretty sharpish up at the Double Star and that from all he could collect, nobody there knew anything much about stock-breeding. He thought it was all fishy. Then again, there is a man who takes stuff there and comes here to rest up. Do you care to guess what they are buying a lot of and having delivered up there?'

'I could not begin to hazard a guess.'

'I will tell you. It was paper! Expensive paper as well. He did not know what they were doing with it, but said that this was not the first lot they had had sent there.'

'That is a regular mystery,' said Farrance. 'Tell me now, why don't you care for the place and its owner?'

'Crawley is an untrustworthy wretch. His men act like they own this town sometimes.'

'Why do people in general tolerate it?'

'There is a lot of money comes to this town from those boys up at the Double Star. As long as they are coming here and spending freely, there is not cause for anybody to ask any awkward questions, you know what I mean?'

'Yes,' said Colonel Farrance. 'I know what you mean.'

* * *

When later that day the colonel met up again with Ikey Wilson, he said, 'Ikey, my boy, I think that we might have found the solution to our problems.'

'How's that?' asked Wilson. 'You mean about getting money out of Andrew Crawley?'

'Out of him or for him. Either way, it will be to your advantage. You might not get your full eleven thousand dollars, but I'll warrant we can get enough for you to buy a little place and settle down on.'

'Well, that sounds good, I will allow,' said Wilson. 'What's to do?'

'I do not recollect whether or not I told you that I was a Justice of the Peace on a part-time basis?'

'You, Bob?' cried Ikey Wilson in amazement. 'That is setting a fox to watch over the hen coop and no mistake. But no, you did not tell me that.'

'Well I am. And as such, I get circulated with a whole heap of printed material such as no normal person could or would wish to read.'

'What sort of stuff are you talking of?'

'A lot of it is to do with taxes and excise and various ordinances of which nobody takes any heed. But mixed in with all that is Wanted notices and also requests for information about crimes.'

'Let me guess, now. Crawley is mixed up in some racket?'

'It could be so, Ikey, it could be so. There is a lot of concern just now in various quarters about counterfeiting operations. Some of the forged bills circulating are as good as the real thing, almost, and efforts are being made to track down the printing presses where these things are being produced.'

'What is that to the present case?'

'It is this. The US Treasury is going mad about this, because it strikes at the very economy. If people lose confidence in the paper currency, then there is a run on gold and all sorts of other bad consequences which lead eventually to banks failing and various other ills. That does not concern us. What does is that Uncle Sam is offering a huge reward for information about such operations. I think that Crawley is up to this game at the Double Star.'

'The deuce you do! Why?'

'I could not make out what we saw unloaded this morning, but after speaking to somebody here in town, I know. It was paper. Very large amounts of it. I hear that they have regular deliveries of good-quality paper up there. Also, we are not the only ones to notice that Crawley is not running a real stud farm.'

'What should we do?'

'First off,' said Farrance, 'is where I want to take a closer look at that ranch, under cover of darkness. I am minded to look in that barn where we saw those packages being carried to.'

'Can't we just go back to Garden City and lay an information against Crawley for counterfeiting?'

'No, not until we are sure in our own minds. I do not want to go off half-cocked, as you might say.'

At something after eleven of the clock on that very night, two shadowy figures might have been seen moving stealthily down the slope behind the Double Star ranch. There were no lookouts or anything of that sort, because as far as any outsiders were concerned, this was no more than a little farming operation. The two men walked slowly and cautiously down towards the outbuildings which were scattered around the main house. Their target was a cattle shed or barn about a hundred yards from the house.

The two of them were carrying stout crowbars and had pistols strapped to their hips. Both hoped that this spying mission might go off smoothly and without any gunplay or bloodshed. Once they had got to the back of the building in which they were interested, the men stopped to see what the next step would be. They wiggled their crowbars into the cracks between some of the planks, but found that it was not possible to gain sufficient purchase to split one plank from another and gain entrance in that way. They accordingly worked their way round to the front of the structure, which faced the house.

'I am hoping to get in here without leaving any sign of entry,' said Farrance. 'I do not wish to spook these boys and make them dig up and leave.'

'I don't look for that,' said Wilson. 'They are nicely settled here. They have been here for better than four years.'

'Yes, there is that. Maybe, even if we do have to break in, they will put it down to sneak thieves or some such.'

It was a dark and moonless night, which meant that there was little chance of anybody in the big house spotting what they were about. The disadvantage was that they could hardly see what they were about in the darkness. After some species of mishandling the thing, Colonel Farrance got a good grip on the padlock which held the door closed. It was a stout one and he had resigned himself to splintering the hasp from the wood in order to gain access, when Ikey Wilson said in a low voice, 'You know what's worth a try, Bob?'

'No,' said the other. 'What might that be?'

'You mind how sometimes we could get locks like that to spring open, just by hitting them hard enough?'

'Why, that's right. I had forgotten such methods. All right, Ikey, you stand clear now while I give it a sharp blow.'

'For God's sake, though, keep the noise down.'

Colonel Robert Farrance, Justice of the Peace in the State of Pennsylvania, prominent and respected businessman, father and various other things, lifted his crowbar and brought it down with a resounding crack upon the padlock. The length of metal hit the lock and scraped along the hasp with a sound like fingernails being drawn down a blackboard. 'Jesus Christ,' said Wilson. 'Will you keep the noise down? I am sure they will have heard that up at the house. Is it open?'

The lock had not opened and so Farrance gave it another whack, which had the desired effect. 'With any luck,' he said, 'we will be able to hang the lock on the door when we have had a look around and those boys will think only that one of them did not lock up properly when last they left.'

The two men entered the barn and closed the door behind them. Farrance lit a stub of candle so that they could gain some idea of what was to be found here. The contents of the building were disappointing in the extreme, consisting of nothing more than vast quantities of paper, most of it wrapped in parcels. One package had been opened and some of the contents removed. The colonel examined the paper carefully and nodded to himself. 'It is just as I thought,' he said to Wilson. 'There can be but one reason for wanting a large amount of this sort of paper.'

After extinguishing the candle, Ikey Wilson and the colonel left the barn only for somebody to open fire upon them as soon as they set foot out of the door. They threw themselves to the ground, so as not to present a silhouette for any murderously minded individual in the vicinity. A couple more shots came their way and they could see that two men with rifles or scatterguns were advancing from the house. 'We're best out of this,' said Farrance. 'Let's just run, but keeping it nice and low.'

The two men ran in a zigzag fashion up the slope, bending double to avoid giving a good target. There did not appear to be any pursuit and there was no further shooting. Wilson said, 'I told you somebody would hear the racket you was making with that padlock.'

'Well, we're still alive, ain't we? Don't take on, it will be fine.' Colonel Farrance was a pretty shrewd judge of such matters; his ability to gauge to a nicety that level of a hazard had been honed over the many years that he had been either an outlaw or soldier. On this occasion, though, his instincts played him false, because they were scarcely back to where they had left the ponies tied up, when they both heard the drumming of hoof beats. They were being pursued by what sounded like at least a half-dozen men.

'What do you say, Bob?' asked Ikey Wilson. 'Do we run or fight?'

'Well, those little ponies of ours are tough enough little beasts for the trail, but I can't see them outrunning big horses such as those sound to be. I reckon it must be fighting.'

Wilson was not in the least dismayed by this news; quite the reverse. He said, 'Well then, let's move from the ponies. I would not want either of them to take a bullet needlessly. Besides which, we are apt to need them when we do decide to leave.'

The trees where the ponies were tethered provided the only sort of cover for some good long way around. Yet Wilson was right, they would need those ponies to get away later and so it made more sense to take the fight to the enemy, rather than allowing the fire of their opponents to rake this area and risk harm to the mounts.

'Well, we had best get clear, then,' said Colonel Farrance. 'Let's run towards them a bit and then lie down.'

They were still on the crest of the rise of ground at back of the ranch and so out of sight yet of those riding up the slope towards them. They sprinted on for a few yards and then fell prone. They were only just in time, because the party of five men came into view at that very moment. Both Farrance and Wilson were still clutching the four-foot-long metal bars that they had thought to use to break into the barn and the glimmering of an idea came to the colonel. He said, 'When I say go, we both jump up and swing our crowbars into one of those men. Then we see what chances.'

'I'm with you,' said Wilson and then the riders were upon them. It was a new moon and the sky was shrouded in dark clouds, so the men on horseback, vainly scanning the horizon for those who had been prying into their secrets, did not think to look down to the ground before them. The first they knew was when two of their number were knocked clean from the saddle by two dark shadows who sprang from the grass ahead of them.

Wilson and the colonel both let out ear-splitting yells as they leaped to their feet and swung the metal bars into the faces of the surprised riders, each taking the man nearest to them. The situation being pretty desperate, they did not stop at one swipe, but battered their targets mercilessly until they fell back, helpless and stunned. The three riders who were not so attacked could not think what to do, because it was impossible to fire in the uncertain light without the risk of hitting the men on their own side. In that respect, the advantage lay with the two men on foot, because they knew clearly who their enemies were: the men on horseback.

Having disabled two of the riders,

both Farrance and Ikey Wilson kept down low behind the horses bearing those whom they had stunned. They drew their pistols and each fired at the men on horseback. One of the riders was killed outright and seeing that they were three men down and not knowing for certain sure how many gunmen they were faced with, the other two turned tail and ran for home, leaving Farrance and Wilson as the victors of the field. They did not waste time congratulating themselves, but simply ran at once to where their ponies were. They mounted and rode off as fast as was practicable and safe, neither wanting to run the risk of laming their mount in the darkness.

When once they were far enough along the track to be reasonably sure of reaching town without being overtaken by men desiring to shed their blood, Wilson said, 'Hell's afire, Bob, that was like a little bit of the good old days! Hot and peppery.'

'Yes,' said the colonel, not altogether displeased himself with how things had turned out. 'I fancy we handled that well enough. Happen the man I tackled will be needing the services of a dental surgeon at some future date. My first blow caught him right in the mouth and I heard those teeth of his breaking.'

'Yeah, I think they will think twice about taking us on again in a hurry.'

'My only fear is that they will now decamp before we have a chance of informing on them.'

'I have been thinking on that,' said Wilson slowly. 'I do not like this scheme of informing. It goes against the grain, as you might say.'

'I dare say it does, but I cannot see any other way that you will be getting any money from that rascal Crawley. It is plain as a pikestaff that he has no intention of paying anything. I wonder if he has the wherewithal, anyway. I guess that he has sunk all his money, and yours too, into that ranch.'

'When you put it like that, then I suppose it will have to be claiming the reward for his capture. Kind of makes me feel like a bounty hunter, though, which is not a comfortable sensation and sits ill with me.'

They spent a final night in the hayloft of the livery stable and in the morning, straight after breakfast, set off back to Garden City.

Both Farrance and Wilson were feeling satisfied with the way that events had panned out. If he was not going to get eleven thousand dollars, then he might get four or five, which would be enough to set him up comfortably. For Colonel Farrance there was the pleasure of thinking that Andrew Crawley might fetch up in a prison cell for a good long time. It was not quite as satisfying to consider as his violent death would have been, but it would do well enough.

Persuading the law in Garden City to get in on the game was a hard row to hoe. The local sheriff refused point blank to touch the case, on the grounds that something involving the Treasury like this was a federal crime and more properly the business of a US Marshal. Nothing that Colonel Farrance said could at first shift him from this blinkered and legalistic view.

'First off,' said Sheriff Giles, 'is where you are quite out of your own jurisdiction, even if you are a Justice of the Peace. Which I have no reason to believe true, in any case.'

'It is not a question of jurisdiction,' said Farrance. 'I am not swearing out a warrant or aught of that sort. Rather, I am laying an information to you about the continuing commission of a felony. It is your duty to enforce the law. You can get together a posse, I suppose?'

'Listen Mr . . . '

'Colonel, if you please,' cut in Farrance, which did not improve the sheriff's temper any.

'Well then colonel,' said Giles, 'I do not need you nor anybody else to come into my office in this way, telling me which way my duty lies. I can gauge that well enough for myself, without outside help.'

'Let us rightly understand each other, sheriff. If you do not act on this information, I am going to go to Topeka and raise hell there. I will make it my life's business to cause you trouble. You will wish you had never been born. Am I making this clear enough for you?'

Sheriff Giles gave this statement some consideration and then went to make another pot of coffee. His natural inclination was to do nothing about this case. It was nothing to him how many fake bills were being printed up by Endeavour. However, he was a good judge of character, if nothing else, and he could tell that this man was trouble. He did not think that he wanted to get crosswise to such a man and have him roaming about the state stirring up bad feeling towards him. He poured out three cups of coffee and took them to where Farrance and his friend were sitting on the other side of his desk.

'If I did undertake to do this, then you and your partner here would have to come with me. I could swear you both in as deputies for the duration. I tell you right now, that I am not even going to contemplate this unless you both agree to that. Anyway, if this turned out to be a snipe hunt, then I want the men who started it close at hand so that I can charge them with some offence or other.'

'You have no business making such a condition and well you know it,' said the colonel, 'but if that is what it takes, then I am content. What do you say, Ikey?'

'Suits me. Long as we get the reward money, that's all I want.'

'Like that, is it?' said Sheriff Giles. 'You sure you boys ain't just common-or-garden bounty hunters?'

'What's it to you?' asked Farrance. 'Your city will not have to pay out the reward. Like you say, this is a federal offence. But it would do your reputation no harm if you were to be the one who brought in the famous counterfeiting gang.'

'Counterfeiting gang!' snorted Giles.

'I don't even know if there is such a thing. I only have your say-so on that.'

Fortunately, Colonel Farrance was possessed of a good and accurate memory. He quoted the number and date of the circular which Sheriff Giles was sure to have received about the counterfeit currency racket that was being investigated. After some searching in a filing cabinet, Giles found the document and laid it on his desk to read. At last, he said, 'I do not recall this at all. Perhaps there is somewhat in this after all. Mind, I still am not promising anything. But you are right, it might not do me harm to be the one to lay hands upon this gang.'

Smelling some sharp practice in the offing, Farrance said, 'We will have it in writing, though, first, that we laid the information in this matter. I do not want to see anybody cheated of reward money.'

'Are you saying that I would swindle you of the reward?' asked Sheriff Giles, his face going pink.

'Such things have been known,' replied Colonel Farrance.

'Well, what do you say?' said the sheriff. 'If I can get the men together, will you come with us?'

Both Farrance and Wilson agreed to this. Really, they were as keen on this arrangement as was the sheriff. Both had the impression that Sheriff Giles might be very ready to take credit for the whole operation and forget later who had given him the information. Before leaving the office, Colonel Farrance drew up an agreement for the sheriff to sign, acknowledging the source of his information. After much huffing and puffing on the part of the lawman, this was signed.

After they left the sheriff's office, Wilson said, 'There is one I would not trust further than I can throw. That man would cheat us as soon as look at us.'

'That was my chief impression too.'

It had been fixed up that Sheriff Giles would set in motion the cumbersome process of raising a posse to raid the Double Star. They were sufficiently far from Endeavour for Farrance not to be worried that word of this would leak out in some way and cause Andrew Crawley and his band to flee. In the meantime, he and Wilson booked into a little hotel and tried to give each other a little room to breathe by going their separate ways during most of the day.

9

The process of raising a posse was somewhat similar to that of calling men for jury service and it was every bit as tiresome and unsatisfactory. Legally, Sheriff Giles could have called upon any able-bodied man in Garden City to aid and assist him in preventing the commission of a crime, but that really only applied to events within the city boundaries. He could, however, summon men to join him in a more protracted expedition, but then the same difficulties were encountered as getting decent men to sit on juries. Those with respectable jobs always had got excuses why they could not be spared, usually claiming that the nature of their employment was such that it was vital to the well-being of the community. The real reason was of course that they did not wish to lose money by sitting around all day in a stuffy courtroom. If this excuse did not serve, then they would invent infirmities such as deafness which would make them unsuitable jurors.

A natural consequence of such shenanigans was that those who did sit on the juries were often loafers and unemployed men who would do it for the nominal payment which they received for the loss of their time. It was even more of a problem getting the right sort of man to join a posse.

Very few family men cared to go haring off for days on end in pursuit of armed and dangerous criminals. There was little point in dragooning men into the thing, because they would then plead poor health, which was all but impossible to disprove. Those who were willing to go off in this fashion were usually young men who were down on their luck. Such types would, at the drop of a hat, engage in looting or theft if you did not watch them the entire time.

Besides which, by 1891, the days of posses chasing desperate men were really over. Most folk looked to the regular law officers to undertake the capture of malefactors. They paid their taxes and wanted to leave the matter in the hands of the authorities.

After four days, Giles and his three deputies had managed to hunt down eight men who would be prepared to ride to Endeavour. With Wilson and Farrance, this would make fourteen men in total, which was not as many as Sheriff Giles would have liked. If it came to trading shots with a band of outlaws, then this could prove a tricky sort of operation altogether.

Wilson, who was enjoying just hanging around and listening to the local gossip, passed on all this information to Colonel Farrance.

'Well, Bob,' he said, after they had been in Garden City for four straight days, 'I think that Giles has finally succeeded in getting together some men. Mind, the word is that these are reckless, stick-at-nothing fellows who are next door to being bandits themselves. Half of them are like that and the other four are loafers who could do with the money. I don't know what will happen if there is hard fighting at the Double Star. I cannot see any of these men hazarding their lives for the sake of the US Treasury!'

'No, that is the way of it when you are paying men to join you in this sort of thing. They will like as not run at the first sound of gunfire.'

'Are you happy to be sworn in as a temporary deputy,' asked Wilson, 'just for the duration, like?'

'Hell, Ikey, I've come this far. I might as well finish the job. I would like to see Andrew Crawley behind bars. You know, I would have given you some money back in Whyteleafe, had you wanted. We did not need to go chasing off in this way.'

'Well now, Bob, I suppose that like you I wanted Crawley to suffer for his past actions. Sure, I want the money, but it will also be good to see Crawley being led off in handcuffs.'

'Isn't that the truth!'

Ikey Wilson laughed and shook his head, as though something had amused him. Colonel Farrance asked what the joke was and Wilson said, 'All this talk about posses has reminded me of that time that you, me and Crawley was being chased. It was in Colorado in the summer of 1859. You remember?'

'Yes, I recall the occasion vividly,' said Farrance, shaking his head in disbelief as he brought the incident to mind. 'I suppose you thought of that because we were talking about the difficulties of getting reliable and courageous men for posses?'

'That is what made me think of it, yes,' said Wilson. 'There we were, racing away from those ten men who were gaining on us slowly but surely, riding over that grassy plain and with nowhere to hide and no means of escape.'

Farrance took up the tale. 'It was Crawley as saved the day. Say what we will of him, nobody ever accused Andrew Crawley of being a coward or being reluctant to fight when the chips were down.'

'That's true enough. Leastways, it was him who suggested what came to be our salvation. He said, 'We are not apt to outrun these boys, so why don't we turn and fight them.''

'And so we did,' said the colonel. 'So we did. Just wheeled round right sudden and rode back towards them with our guns blazing. I reckon that most of those boys were only there for the payment. Leastways, they did not seem none too keen on facing us. Every man Jack of them fled.'

'They did, by God. The whole parcel of them just turned tail and ran for cover. Three of us against ten of them. I guess their nerve was broke, because they did not take up the pursuit again after we set off once more.'

'No,' said Farrance. 'I recollect that they did not, which was a curious thing when I look back upon it. After we had scattered them, they just seemed to give up any further idea of taking us.'

'I cannot deny,' said Wilson, 'that Crawley played the man that day, whatever he has done since.'

'In fairness to him, I will say this. If you had your tail in a crack and the going was tough, then you could not hope for a better man at your side than Andrew Crawley. He made a damned good outlaw.'

Wilson smiled and said, 'Question is, will the two of us make as good lawmen as we did outlaws? It will be strange to ride on the right side of the law. Especially me, just not that long out of gaol.'

'If I can become a Justice of the Peace, Ikey, then I dare say that you will be able to serve as a deputy sheriff for a few days. It is odd how life turns out. Who would have thought that one day we two would be riding with the law against our old partner?'

* * *

There was a good deal of interest in Garden City at the sight of an old-style posse riding out of town. For children, this was a regular novelty — something which they had never seen before. The fourteen riders assembled throughout the morning outside the sheriff's office. They blocked up the road and generally made a lot of themselves, the younger members of the band swaggering and making great show of displaying their firearms. A crowd gathered on the sidewalk to watch the unusual spectacle and folk said that it was just like a bit of the old days.

Sheriff Giles was not altogether displeased at the effect his posse was having upon the citizens of Garden City. He knew full well that there were any number of taxpayers who were of the opinion that he was a lazy old bastard who was barely worth his keep, the crime rate in that town being very low. This would show them, though — he and his deputies going off fifty miles to apprehend a dangerous gang of crooks. Giles made a great show of shouting instructions and bustling around importantly in his role as peace officer.

In fact, some members of the town council had raised objections to the expedition to Endeavour on the grounds that this was quite beyond the jurisdiction of their own sheriff who, if he had time to spare, might start to spend more of his waking hours enforcing such things as building ordinances. However, when the sheriff had explained the advantages to them of the famous gang of counterfeiters being caught by their sheriff, when the US Treasury had been after them for a good long while with no success, they too began to see the good points of the case. At the very least, it would be good publicity for Garden City and indicate to the nation that the west of Kansas was no longer outlaw country.

Colonel Farrance cast an appraising look over the men who were gathered outside Sheriff Giles's office. He shared Ikey Wilson's misgivings in no small measure. Three of these men hardly looked old enough to be shaving yet and had probably volunteered so that they would have something to boast about for the next few months. One man was so ancient that if he had not been on horseback, Farrance would have expected him to be in a wheelchair or hobbling down the road with the aid of a walking stick. Presumably he was trying to recapture the glories of his youth. At a guess, the others were unemployed loafers who made money in whatever way seemed easiest. They looked like men who might have an easy facility with firearms, though, which was in truth the only thing that was needful on an outing of this sort.

'What do you make of them?' asked Wilson in a low voice.

'Much the same as you, I should think, Ikey,' replied Farrance. 'They look a pretty feeble and uninspiring crew. Who in God's name let that old boy join the ride?'

'You mean Methuselah?' said Wilson, grinning. 'You know, I don't know but that he might be the most useful of the lot. He is keen as mustard and by all accounts is the best shot in the county. I would sooner have him by my side than those boys. Why, they don't look like their balls have dropped yet.'

'I too thought so,' said Colonel Farrance. 'I suppose that we should be glad that Giles has organized anything at all, but I do not have a good feeling about this. What about you?'

'I am content that there are others to support us, Bob. We managed the other night to take on five riders and us on foot and still we came out on top. As I see it, we will probably end up doing the lion's share of this job by our own selves. Still and all, we stand to collect the reward money and so that is perhaps fair.'

* * *

At about noon, the posse rode off. There was among those watching a sense that this was a spectacle whose day had passed and some of the older watchers said to one another that they did not expect to see such an event as this again. The men riding behind Sheriff Giles also had an awkward and self-conscious air about them, as though they too realized that there was something archaic and faintly ridiculous about the whole thing. Fortunately, Garden City was in the main a law-abiding and peaceful place and the loss of its sheriff for a few days was not likely to be the signal for widespread crime and disorder.

'You know,' said the colonel, speaking privately to Wilson as they moved towards the edge of town, 'it might be no bad thing if we two decided how we are going to play this.'

'I am glad to hear you say that,' said Wilson. 'I don't think you told me the exact terms of the reward.'

'It relates to information provided to

the law which then leads to the apprehension or death of those responsible for the counterfeiting.'

'Or death,' said Wilson, meditatively. 'That sounds all right. Meaning that they will pay out if Crawley and his boys are all killed?'

'If the evidence warrants it, yes.'

'Like, if they find printing presses and plates for dollar bills and suchlike?'

'That's it. We have provided the information and if it leads to the capture or death during arrest of those behind the operation, well then the government will pay out.'

'I hope that I will get a chance to face Crawley man to man,' said Wilson. 'I would like to be able to settle with him in a fair fight.'

'I would not look for that to happen here. There are too many people involved. Do not be shooting Crawley. That sheriff may be a fool but he will not put up with that sort of thing. He will be wanting to ride back into Garden City with a heap of prisoners.'

The party of men camped for the night some ten miles from Endeavour. As Sheriff Giles said, it would be good to get up in the morning bright and early and then ride straight down onto the ranch and take them unawares. After giving this short speech, he took Farrance and Wilson to one side and had a few private words with them.

'I do not ask what game you two are up to,' said Giles. 'I do not know and nor do I want to. It may be the reward money, but I guess there is more to it than that.'

Neither Wilson nor the colonel felt called upon to offer any further explanation, notwithstanding the fact that the sheriff looked at them expectantly, as though he was waiting for them to speak. When the silence had stretched out long enough to be a mite embarrassing, he continued, 'Well, you are both going to keep your own counsel and there is nothing more to be said on that topic. Touching upon how we approach this place, do you have any ideas?'

Farrance set mind to this question for a second or two and then said, 'There is an old Indian trail running north from Endeavour to the Double Star. If you wish to avoid giving any warning by passing through the town, then we could head a little north from here and then strike into the trail some way from Endeavour.'

'Is that what you would recommend?' asked Giles. 'I will not deny that I have not taken part in anything quite like this before, not out in open country. I am used to operating in town.'

'Are you asking me how I would play it?' said Colonel Farrance. 'Because if so, I will willingly assist you to the best of my ability.'

'Say that I am, then. What would you do?'

It was tolerably clear to both Wilson and Farrance that the sheriff, right out of his depth here, was pumping them for ideas, which he would then represent to the others as having proceeded from his own brain. This was fine by them, as long as it worked towards their own ends.

'Then, I would suggest . . . ' said Farrance, very hesitantly, like he did not wish to step over the boundaries of what was right and proper or take to himself leadership of the expedition. 'Why not send four or five men to present themselves at the front door and demand entrance. While these men are engaging those in the ranch house, the rest of us will be taking up good firing positions around the place, so that if it comes to fighting, we have the advantage.'

'That sounds well enough,' said Sheriff Giles, 'but I am not sure of finding volunteers to march right up to the house like that. What if they are shot down at once?'

'Me and my partner will do it, if you can find two others,' was the reply.

'You have balls, colonel,' said the sheriff. 'I will give you that. I will see if two of my deputies will go along up to the door with you. What if they start shooting at you? What then?'

'Let's take it a day at a time,' said Farrance. 'Have you not heard where it says in scripture, 'Sufficient unto the day is the evil thereof, give ye therefore no thought to the morrow'?'

'I did not have you pegged for the religious type.'

When the sheriff wandered off to talk to the other men and while everybody was gathering up bits of wood to light fires and get coffee going, Wilson said, 'You surely opened your mouth wide there, Bob. Why the hell did you want to volunteer us for that little job? Weren't you in the army, like me? Don't you know that the first rule of being a soldier is that you never volunteer for anything?'

Colonel Farrance chuckled. 'I had not heard that rule, I will confess. Is that why we officers always found it so damned hard to find people for various little jobs? But that's nothing to the purpose. There is another rule that you might have come across in your life. I learned it at my mother's knee, these sixty years past. It is this: if you want a job done properly, you must do it yourself.'

'Ah, I take you. Meaning, I suppose, that if we rely on that fool of a sheriff, the affair will miscarry.'

'Yes,' said Farrance. 'And we will end up with no prisoners or reward money for you.'

'What, then, when we go for to ride up to that place? Suppose Crawley's boys do just shoot at us?'

'I don't look for that. With four of us arriving at once, they will come out to see what's what. There's no reason for them to start blasting away at us at once. I don't think the risk is great.'

After they had eaten the rations they brought with them, Wilson and the colonel wrapped blankets around themselves and settled down for the night. The other members of the posse were crowded together and talking over the possible outcomes of the arrests. They kept casting glances at the two older men who seemed so self-contained and apparently needing no company. Wilson said, 'They think we are odd fishes.'

'Maybe they are right. It is the damnedest thing to find myself doing this after all these years.'

'Will that daughter of yours be all right in your absence?' asked Wilson suddenly.

'Charlotte? Yes, there is my housekeeper to take care of her and also the tutors will be coming in. She will be well enough until I get back.'

'Do you miss her?'

'That's a blazing odd question, Ikey. Was there ever the father of a sixteen-year-old girl who was not glad to get away from her from time to time? I dare say she will be glad of the break from my presence.'

'She is a real nice girl. I could tell when first she met me, she did not know what to make of it. But she is a natural born lady and soon treated me like anybody else.'

'Why, you fool,' said Farrance, roughly. 'You are like anybody else, aren't you? You are just a little down on your luck is all. We are soon to remedy that. Hush now, for I wish to sleep.'

Long after the colonel had dozed off and while the rest of the posse were talking and laughing around their fires, Ikey Wilson lay awake, staring up at the stars.

For some eleven or twelve years now, hardly anybody had treated him as a real human being. Certainly not in gaol, and since his release he had been no more than a vagrant. People might afford him a little cold charity, but that was more for the sake of their own souls than out of any genuine concern for him as a person. Bob Farrance was being decent to him, but that was because he felt guilty for his own past, not because he really liked Wilson or wanted him as a friend. Charlotte Farrance alone had responded to him as a real person, somebody deserving of respect and to be treated with kind interest. As such, the young woman stood out in the world for Ikey Wilson and he would have done anything in his power to help the girl or protect her from harm.

As he moved restlessly, unable to sleep, Ikey Wilson asked himself what he would really like out of life now that he was free again. The answer was simple. He would like to have a little patch of land and a house of his own. More than that, he would like to have a wife and children of his own. Maybe a little girl who would grow into a fine, kind person like Bob Farrance's daughter.

10

It was the finest, brightest morning that Farrance could ever remember. Maybe that was in part because he was not in the habit of being up at this time of year in time to see the dawn break on the open country. The sky was still a dark — almost violet — blue and the sun a vivid red line as thin as a nail paring above the distant hills.

It may have been summer, but it was chilly enough first thing in the morning when you are sleeping out under the sky. There was much coughing and swearing as Sheriff Giles went round the camp, waking all the men in a fairly rough fashion. He sounded edgy and in a bad humour, which the colonel attributed to his nerves. I bet it's a good long while, he thought to himself, since you faced the prospect of hostile fire from desperate men. Giles wanted the credit of breaking up the gang of forgers all right, but he surely did not like the preliminary activities which went with that honour; in this case riding into the lair of a bunch of stick-at-nought roughnecks. It would be curious to see how he handled the matter as the day progressed.

Wilson was very quiet as he brewed up the coffee and Colonel Farrance tried to cheer him up by joshing him about his supposed fear of action. 'I am surprised at you, Ikey, to see you in such a condition with your nerves over the prospect of setting to with a scoundrel like Crawley. Why, the time was that you would not have thought twice about going against any man living.'

His words had some effect, because Wilson growled, 'Crawley? For ten cents I'd tear his liver out and eat it raw. Crawley!'

'Well then, what ails you? Have you slept well?'

'Not overmuch. Let me be now, Bob.

I have been thinking a deal about my life and the reckoning won't come out straight.'

'Considering the life you have led, that is not to be wondered at,' said Farrance, which at least raised the ghost of a smile on the other man's face.

Sheriff Giles came over to speak with them after everybody had had coffee and whatever other vittles they had left over from the night before. He said, 'You will lead us to this Indian trail? And then you and your partner will go up to the house while we take up our positions back of the place?'

'If two men will ride with us, yes,' replied Farrance. 'Not else.'

'That's all arranged. One of my boys will go along with you and also Mr Beauregarde.'

'Beauregarde?' said Wilson. 'Which of the crew might bear such a fancy name as that?'

'There he is,' said Giles, pointing out the man. 'He is setting over yonder by his self.'

Wilson said, 'You mean Methuselah? Come, he is old as the hills. It would not be fair on him or us. Will none of the younger men come with us?'

Sheriff Giles looked a little sheepish. 'It is this way,' he explained. 'Two of my deputies are married and have their wives and children to think on. Jim Sellars is young and single and game for anything. He is a tough one all right. As for old Mr Beauregarde, do not be deceived by his aged appearance. He is the very devil and cares nothing about his life. He will not be displeased to go down in a blaze of gunfire this day. I had it in strictest confidence that his doctor has found some growth in him which is like to kill him in a few months. He has nothing to lose.'

After Giles had moved on to chivvy up some of the more sluggish members of the band, Wilson said to the colonel, 'This is a fine state of affairs. It looks to me as though that bastard will have us doing all the work and taking all the danger. Just look at that old boy; he must be a hundred.'

'Go and fetch him over, Ikey. Let's get to know him a little and see if he will be any use to us if the going gets lively.'

Old Mr Beauregarde was stone deaf and extremely peppery. He came and sat with the other two and listened to what they had to say of their plans. Then he announced bluntly, 'I ain't got but till this year's end to live. I'm not aiming to die in some damned hospital ward, screaming with pain.'

'Well, Mr Beauregarde,' interrupted Colonel Farrance courteously. 'That is all well and good . . . '

'Don't give me all that flannel, boy,' said Mr Beauregarde. 'I don't have the patience. You want to knock at the door, all fine by me. If those boys start shooting, then you and the other fellow can ride off and leave me. I ain't afraid of them and will draw their fire. Cover your retreat, like.'

Even Ikey Wilson, who was the least squeamish of men and had been mixed up in his fair share of coldblooded tricks, could not stomach this notion. He said, 'Begging your pardon, sir, but that won't answer. Nobody's leaving anybody anywhere.' He spoke lightly but with great feeling, perhaps recalling the time thirty years earlier when he had himself been abandoned to his fate in the course of a fierce gun battle. 'No,' he continued, 'it won't do. We will all ride together and nobody will be sacrificed.'

'You young fool,' said Mr Beauregarde with the greatest irascibility. 'I want to be killed by a bullet. What's wrong with you?'

Wilson looked coldly at the stubborn old man and said, 'You got a gun there. You want to die by a bullet, then shoot yourself right now. You got no business making a murderer of some stranger.'

Farrance smoothed things over by saying, 'Let's just agree that we will all go openly to the ranch house and see what develops, Mr Beauregarde. It may not come to any shooting.'

The old man stood up and spat a stream of tobacco juice into the fire. 'I'll ride along of you two if you've no objection? On the way there, that is to say.' Without waiting to hear their assent to this proposition, he stumped off; looking, as Wilson had remarked the previous day, as though he would be better in a wheelchair.

The sun had changed from dull red to burning gold before they were fairly on their way. It was only a ten-mile ride, but there seemed no reason to proceed at anything other than a gentle trot. The way was not straight and although it was only ten miles as the crow flies, the posse travelled half as much again by weaving back and forth along the undulating landscape.

After an hour and a half, they struck the Indian path that Wilson and Farrance had used when they made their night-time visit to the Double Star. Colonel Farrance rode up to Sheriff Giles and said, 'This is where we turn right and keep going for perhaps three miles, until we come out on a rise of ground overlooking the ranch.'

'How do you expect to find them? Do you think they will be prepared for trouble?'

'I don't know,' said Farrance, 'and that's the God's honest truth. My partner and me might have stirred up the hornets' nest, if you wish to put it so, a few nights back. I would think that they will have settled down again by now.'

'Well then,' said Giles. 'Do you four who are going to ride down on them want to lead the way? You know the lie of the land. When we are nigh to the place, tell me and we can split into different parties.' He paused for a moment and then said in a rush, 'This is the hell of a thing. Aren't you at all nervous?'

Colonel Farrance didn't smile; he had no wish to shame the man, especially in front of others. Instead, he said gently, 'We all get a bit jumpy before action. It is nothing to speak of.'

When he rejoined Wilson and the other two men, Farrance told them that Sheriff Giles wanted them to lead the way. Upon hearing this, Mr Beauregarde said loudly, 'Yellow, is he? Wants us to do his own job.' Several of the younger men heard this and grinned to themselves.

After another hour of walking their mounts carefully along the track, they came nigh to where Colonel Farrance and Ikey Wilson had had the night-time set-to with five of the men from the Double Star. Looking at the rugged trail by broad light of day, Farrance wondered how in the hell he and Wilson had ridden so fast along it in the dark without breaking their necks. He stopped and indicated to the rest of the posse to wait up.

'We are now within a short distance of the ranch,' said Colonel Farrance. 'Sheriff Giles is going to lead most of you fellows round the back of the house, while me and these others are going to walk our horses down to the front and acquaint them with the circumstances.'

'Meaning what?' said the youngest of the men.

'Meaning,' said Farrance, 'that me and others will approach the house peacefully and desire those within to yield up their ordinance and consider themselves our prisoners. To put the case in military parlance, that is.'

Sheriff Giles had an inkling that he ought himself to be the one making any fancy speeches upon the occasion and said, 'Right, according to the colonel here, we must go round to the right here and work our way to the rear of the house. He, Sellars, Beauregarde and Wilson will cut along to the left and ride straight down to the front door.'

When the two parties had divided, Farrance said to Mr Beauregarde, 'I would be obliged sir, if you would not start any shooting and just take your lead from me. The same goes for you too, Mr Sellars. Me and Wilson here will decide if and when it is time to fight.'

Deputy Sellars, who might reasonably have believed himself to be in charge of the group, seemed content to allow the colonel to assume command. He was a young man, with even less experience of this kind of thing than his boss. Once they were over the crest of the hill, the ranch and its outbuildings and surrounding patchwork of fields was laid out beneath them. They could see Sheriff Giles and the others working their way round to the right in a flanking manoeuvre. There was no sign of life on the ranch and Farrance hoped for everybody's sake that he had not led them all on a snipe hunt. It would be a poor show after all this performance if they were to descend upon the place and find nobody at home.

As they reached the foot of the slope and began walking their horses to the house, Colonel Farrance came up with a better explanation for why there was no sign of life. They had been up at dawn and started on the trail soon after. Despite their own feelings of the morning being half gone, it was no more than seven or eight. It was entirely possible that those in the house had not even risen yet.

'What do you make of it, Bob?' asked Wilson. 'Reckon there's anybody at home?'

'Hard to say. The horses are still in the fields and corrals, so I am thinking that they have not all lit out.'

'Yes,' said Wilson. 'I too noticed that. What will we do if nobody comes out before we get to the house? I do not fancy dismounting and knocking on the door.'

They had now reached the low stone wall in front of the ranch house. There was a gap in this wall opposite the front door and no gate to hinder them from riding right into the yard in front of the house; which they did. And still, the noise of their horses did not bring anybody out to investigate.

'It is time to draw and cock our

pieces,' said Farrance, 'but let no man fire a shot unless we are first shot at.' He turned and faced Old Man Beauregarde and said loudly, 'Do you mark what I say, Mr Beauregarde? No shooting yet.'

'All right, all right,' said the old man querulously, 'I ain't as deaf as all that. I heard you well enough.' These were the last words that the old man ever spoke in the whole course of his life, because he had no sooner finished the sentence than there was the crack of a rifle shot and old Mr Beauregarde gave a grunt and toppled sideways from the saddle with half his head shot away.

'Out of here!' cried Farrance and wheeled his horse around as another shot echoed across the yard. 'Ride to that barn.' He matched the words to the action and rode hell for leather towards the nearby barn, cantering round the side of it for shelter. Wilson and Deputy Sellars also reached the safety of the stone walls a second or two later.

'Goddam,' said Wilson angrily. 'They

did not even wait to hear what we had to say.'

Colonel Farrance burst out laughing at that. 'What would you have, Ikey? They know it's a raid and are not prepared to go tamely to gaol for twenty years or more. I don't know that I blame them.'

'Yes, I know, but still and all, that old gentleman. It is a bit much.'

'Think on this,' said Farrance. 'At least now we know that they are here and up to some villainy. Least we are sure to catch or kill them.'

'First catch your hare,' said Wilson. 'Those boys look pretty determined to me not to be taken.'

Sellars, the young deputy, was looking shaky and pale at this turn of events. He had been right next to Mr Beauregarde when the old man had been killed and this had taken him aback. Farrance said, 'You all right there, feller? Don't take on so; the old man was not sorry to die. Fact is, I think that is why he volunteered for this exercise in the first instance, so that he could find an easier death than he might have done through his cancer.'

'It's still the hell of the thing,' said Sellars. 'I never saw the like.'

Wilson chipped in, saying, 'Don't set mind to it. Stick close to me and my partner and we will see you safe through this.'

While all this was taking place right in front of the ranch house, Sheriff Giles and the other nine men had been crawling towards the house like Indians and taking up firing positions at the back. As soon as the shooting started, which resulted in the death of the old man, some members of the posse commenced firing at the windows at the back of the house. There was no return fire and after a space, those under the command of the sheriff ceased fire to see what would chance.

'This won't do,' muttered Farrance. 'That damned fool of a sheriff has no idea how to proceed further. We will be here until nightfall at this rate.' He went to the corner of the barn and shouted loudly, 'Crawley, you are surrounded, man. Throw down your weapons and come out with your hands up. I promise that you will be treated well and taken for a fair trial.'

The response from inside the house was a few well-aimed shots which caused Colonel Farrance to dodge swiftly back behind the shelter of the stone wall of the barn.

'What do you say to taking a more active part in this?' the colonel said to Wilson. 'Meaning, how about us two getting a little closer in while Deputy Sellars here offers us covering fire?'

'Come on, then,' replied Wilson. 'I would rather be moving than cowering behind a wall like this.'

Turning to Sellars, Colonel Farrance said, 'Can you start firing at the windows a little to keep those boys from peering out and getting a bead on us?'

'You want I should come with you?' asked the deputy, although it was obvious he had no appetite for such a course of action and was asking only for form's sake.

'No, you would be a sight more use to us here, son,' said Farrance. 'We need you to keep those boys occupied.'

While Sellars kept the men in the house busy with constant fire and drew in turn their own fire to the corner of the barn where he was positioned, Wilson and Farrance ran to the other end of the barn and emerged from the opposite corner at a run, throwing themselves behind a low wall which was only fifty feet or so from the side of the house.

'Think they know we're here?' asked Wilson. 'Nobody has shot at us.'

'No, I wouldn't have thought so. They are too busy with yon deputy to have noticed us appear in another spot. You know yourself what it is like in these cases: you focus only upon the immediate danger.'

Wilson poked his head above the wall. 'There is no window overlooking us here. What say we run for the side wall of the house and see where that leaves us?'

From the sound of it, the shooting was not just between Deputy Sellars and the men in the house. There was rifle fire from the left, which indicated to Wilson and Farrance that the sheriff and his men were drawing nearer and perhaps also getting ready to move in on the house.

'Let's go, then,' said Farrance, jumping up and running to the house. He and Wilson sprinted as fast as they were able, fearing at any moment to receive a bullet for their pains. Nothing happened, though, and it looked as though Wilson had been right and they were in a blind spot.

Sheriff Giles and his men were engaging in duels from the cover of walls, popping up to fire and then dropping out of sight again. In between times, Colonel Farrance noted approvingly that they were slowly drawing nearer to the house. There came a lull in the firing and then he and Wilson recognized Andrew Crawley's voice calling out from a window. He cried, 'Hold your fire. I see there are too many of you there. Me and my boys will come out with our hands high. Just don't be shooting us out of hand when we are in your power.'

Sheriff Giles shouted back, and the relief was evident in his voice. 'Nobody will be shooting any prisoners. If you surrender now, then I will take you all back to stand trial for whatever it is you have been up to.' It sounded to Wilson and Farrance that the sheriff was mightily relieved that he would not be called upon further to hazard his own person.

Wilson whispered to the colonel, 'Crawley's bluffing. He never surrendered in his life. He would sooner die.'

'That's how I read the case as well. Since all the attention is on the back of the house now, why don't we set mind to what is happening at this end?'

From the back of the house came

Crawley's voice again, calling from the window. 'Here come our weapons, now!' There was a clatter of guns being thrown out the windows at back of the house, then Crawley said, 'All right, we're coming out now. We will leave by the kitchen door, nigh to where you and your men are. All of us will have our hands above our heads.'

'Here we go,' said Wilson. 'I'll warrant that while his men are trooping out of that back door, Crawley will make a bolt from the front and hope to evade capture.' So it proved, for in the next second, they saw a figure come flying from the front door of the ranch house, heading straight towards the field where there were horses grazing. Both Farrance and Wilson were after him in an instant and brought him to the ground before he had left the yard. Wilson relieved the furiously struggling man of the pistol clenched in his hand, by the simple expedient of stamping on his wrist. At this point, Deputy Sellars realized that there was some glory to be had and came scuttling out from behind the barn, so that he could appear to have been involved in the arrest.

So awful was the language used by Crawley as he fought to free himself that Colonel Farrance said sternly, 'Recollect yourself, Andrew. I'll take oath that this young deputy has not heard the half of those curse-words that you are using so freely. You will corrupt his morals.'

Crawley stopped struggling and looked directly into Farrance's eyes. He held the other man's gaze for a moment and then said quietly, 'I will be revenged upon you for this, Bob. I will make sure that you regret this day's business for the whole of your life, I promise you that. I will do it though it cost me my own life.'

'Hush your mouth now, you damned fool,' said Wilson. 'You are being unmanly. In the old days we would not have threatened one another so.'

Crawley turned to Wilson and said,

'You too, Ikey. I will see you in hell for this.'

In addition to Crawley, there were another eight men taken prisoner. Sheriff Giles was insufferable in victory, representing himself as the master brain who had organized and executed the entire raid single-handed. Once the men from the house were unarmed, he was very active in seeing that they were handcuffed and roped together to render escape impossible.

The house proved to contain a printing press, bales of paper and a vast quantity of forged paper money. It was certainly the base of the counterfeiting racket that had so exercised the minds of those in the Treasury. At the discovery of this evidence, Giles was cock-a-hoop. He said jovially to the colonel, 'I will allow that I owe you for this. I shouldn't wonder if it didn't make my name sir, make my name!'

'What will you do with the prisoners?' enquired Farrance. 'Will you take them straight back to Garden City? I tell you now, you need to set a watch upon Crawley, who is the leader of the outfit.'

'I do not need anybody to teach me my job,' said the sheriff stiffly. 'Since you ask, we are going to stay over first at Endeavour. I am sure that I can find safe lodgings for them there.'

The journey to Endeavour was not a pleasant one for the men taken at the Double Star. The posse rode and the men they had captured had to proceed on foot, it being too much trouble to saddle up horses for them, not to mention the risk of an escape bid. This way, they were all roped together and there was no chance of any one, bold fellow making a bolt for it.

The party took just under three hours to get to the town and their arrival created a minor sensation, with people coming out of their homes to see what was going on. It was certainly no common sight: eleven men on horseback leading a line of nine footsore men, all jangling handcuffs and roped together like a chain gang. Most of these prisoners were known in the town for their free-spending habits and drunken antics.

There was no lawman in Endeavour and so Sheriff Giles found to his pleasure that he was able to throw his weight about to no small extent. He commandeered a barn at the livery stable, offering the owner unspecified recompense from government funds for the present inconvenience to which he was put. All the men taken captive at the Double Star were herded into this and the door locked. Giles set two of his own deputies to guard, with another two of the posse patrolling nearby.

The problem now for the sheriff was getting these apprehended miscreants safely back to Garden City. It was impossible that they should be able to walk all that way; the logistics of the thing were too tricky. He had left two of the men back at the Double Star to guard the evidence of counterfeiting and it now seemed that he would have to send a few more men back to the ranch to collect horses. The only option was for the prisoners to ride alongside their captors for a couple of days, a prospect which Sheriff Giles viewed with no enthusiasm whatsoever. As it turned out, by the next day there were only four prisoners to transport east, which made the job a little less arduous. Here is what happened.

Farrance had all along been uneasy about the casual way that the sheriff was dealing with a dyed-in-the-wool villain like Andrew Crawley. He could hardly say too much about the man, for fear of revealing his own disreputable past, but he knew that Crawley was a good deal worse than any mere forger of currency. Still, there it was; he had tried to warn Giles and been soundly rebuffed and told, in effect, to mind his own affairs.

The first that Colonel Farrance knew of any trouble was while he was walking around just outside the town, enjoying the night air and solitude. He was beginning to feel that he had had about enough of these adventures now to last him for the rest of his life and he would be glad to get back to Whyteleafe and his daughter just as soon as ever he was able. These peaceful reflections were broken by the sound of shooting from the centre of town and Farrance knew, without the least shadow of a doubt, that this meant that Crawley was on the loose. It was irrational; he just knew it as sure as God made little apples. He drew the Remington from its holster and set off towards the livery stable as fast as his legs would carry him.

The shooting surged to a crescendo and then tailed off into a few scattered, single shots. By the time he got to the barn where the men had been held, it was all over.

As he neared the livery stable, a man with a rifle jumped out and, seeing the pistol in his hand, cried, 'Stand to and drop that weapon!' Then, recognizing the colonel, he said, 'Belay that, I see it's you, sir.' The speaker was one of

Sheriff Giles's deputies and he was as worked up and on edge as could be. This was caused partly by the death of his friend, Jim Sellars, who was lying in the dust near the livery stable.

'What happened?' asked Farrance of the deputy.

'My partner Jim, which is to say Jim Sellars, was guarding the barn with me. One of those inside called out that a man was sick and needed a doctor. Jim went in and was jumped by a few of those bastards. They half strangled him and took his gun. Then when he ran out to raise the alarm, they shot him in the back. Bastards!'

'What's the case now?'

'Me and some of the other boys opened fire to halt their flight,' said the deputy, daring Colonel Farrance to contradict him, 'and some were killed. Four remain alive and one man has got away.'

'That would be Andrew Crawley,' said the colonel flatly. 'I knew this would happen.'

The deputy stared hard at Farrance and said, 'You seem to know an awful lot about this sort of wickedness. Sheriff thinks you are not entirely as you represent yourself to be.'

'That's nothing,' said Farrance. 'How come you killed four of those prisoners? Were none wounded?'

'No,' said the deputy. 'They was all killed.'

Colonel Farrance could work out easy enough what had taken place and as it happened, he was quite correct in his calculations. The deputy had arrived just as Crawley, the only escaping prisoner with a gun, had vanished into the darkness. Seeing his partner lying there dead, the deputy had then turned his gun on the milling crowd of prisoners, eight men who could not quite make up their minds whether to run for it or stay put. He had shot four of them out of hand, before Sheriff Giles had come upon the scene and prevented a wholesale massacre.

'You will not have any problems with

these four men now,' said Farrance. 'Like as not they will be too scared to stir an inch.'

'They would be wise,' said the deputy, 'to be that way. I would cheerfully shoot the rest of them.'

At this point, Ikey Wilson came ambling up and asked what was to do with all the shooting. He too was a little taken aback to see five corpses and just like the colonel, he soon figured out what had happened. He and Farrance walked off a space, down the road. Wilson said, 'You look awful worried, Bob. What ails you? You are not thinking about Andrew Crawley now, are you?'

'Why, yes,' said Farrance. 'That is precisely so. I am wondering where he has gone now.'

'That don't signify, surely? As long as they have caught and killed some, the reward still stands, doesn't it?'

'It might not signify to you, Ikey,' said Farrance, a touch of irritation in his voice, 'and yes, you will still get the reward. I am wondering where that rascal has got to, nonetheless. He threatened vengeance upon me and you, if you recall.'

'But I don't get it, Bob. How could he harm either of us now?'

'I don't rightly know, but I am not easy in my mind about this. Not easy at all.'

Later that night, Colonel Farrance tried to reason through the case in his mind. There had been a gap of some days between him and Wilson leaving Endeavour and their returning at the head of a posse. Would Crawley have been in town during that time? Could he have asked around about Farrance and Wilson? He recollected vaguely that he had mentioned to more than one person that he lived in Pennsylvania. He was well enough known in that state that anybody fetching up in Harrisburg, say, would be able to get a line on him by asking round a bit. It would not be a difficult task to track him to Whyteleafe.

But surely, he was being over

anxious? Having escaped from justice, wouldn't Crawley's efforts now be concentrated upon fleeing and saving his own life? Then again, Farrance had more or less wrecked the man's life here. From owning a large ranch and being a wealthy and important person, due to his interference, Andrew Crawley was now a desperate fugitive from justice; and since the escape, one facing the rope if apprehended for the murder of a peace officer.

11

There was more delay before the much-reduced party of men was ready to leave for Garden City. Horses had to be collected from the Double Star, provisions acquired for the journey and various other arrangements made. Colonel Farrance was unable to shake off the feelings of impending disaster which gripped him when his thoughts turned to Crawley. Wilson tried to cheer him along, but he just knew that some mischief was afoot in that direction.

Before they started out for Garden City, the twelve men of the posse, four prisoners and two corpses of the men who had been killed in the lawful execution of their duty, Sheriff Giles addressed the prisoners thus:

'You cowsons have killed two good men. Old Mr Beauregarde and my deputy, Jim Sellars. I tell you now, that when we get back to my town, I shall be charging all four of you with the murder of a peace officer. That breakout was a joint enterprise and every man Jack of you will hang for it.'

One of the men tried to interrupt, intending perhaps to offer some justification or excuse, but Giles would have none of it. 'Shut your mouth, you bastard,' he said. 'You are lucky that I do not hang all of you right now. I am strongly minded to, I'll tell you that for nothing.'

The possibility of a lynching had occurred to the others and when the man who had tried to speak looked about to say something, they jogged him in the ribs and told him to keep quiet. They knew that it would not take much for the sheriff to string them up right then and there.

The bodies of the four outlaws were left in Endeavour and the sheriff promised to send on money to pay for their burial. As they rode out of town,

Sheriff Giles got alongside Farrance and said, 'You and your partner will be wanting to know about the reward money. I will vouch for the capture and so on. It will take a little time but if you like, I can arrange for it to be paid out where you are resident. Pennsylvania, wasn't it?'

'Yes, that is so. If I gave you a telegraphic address, I guess that might expedite matters?'

In short, once they had got back safely to Garden City, there was no need for Colonel Farrance and Ikey Wilson to hang around. They would be paid a sum for having ridden with the posse and their duties would be ended.

After the sheriff had moved off, the colonel said to Wilson, 'I suppose you had best come back to Whyteleafe with me, Ikey. It will take a time for that reward money to come through and I would not have you sleeping rough until then.' The truth was that he had grown kind of fond of Wilson in a funny sort of way over the last few weeks and the idea of having the man in his house for a time was not as irksome as all that. So it was that two days after arriving in Garden City, Farrance and Wilson began the long railroad journey from Kansas to Pennsylvania.

It was a great relief to Farrance to reach Whyteleafe after all his recent adventures and purely a delight to see his beloved daughter again. Being only sixteen, she had not yet acquired that veneer of a well-bred lady, which manifests itself in a complete lack of interest in masculine affairs. Indeed, she was openly and avidly curious about what her father and Mr Wilson had been up to. She artfully tried every blandishment upon her father and various species of coquetry upon Wilson in order to extract information about their recent whereabouts — all to no avail. The two men asserted boldly that they had just been on a little vacation, the details of which could be of no possible interest to a young thing like her.

Farrance and Wilson sat talking late that first night, after Charlotte had retired for the night.

'It's right good of you to let me stay here until this reward money is arranged,' said Wilson. 'I wouldn't have looked for it and it is appreciated.'

'Hell, Ikey, we have had a good time. I don't suppose consulting all my ledgers and so on, which is what I would have been doing had you not showed up here, would have been as entertaining as what we have been up to. Stay as long as you want. Anyways, Charlotte seems to like having you around.'

Just after dawn the next day, Colonel Farrance was awakened from sleep by a piercing shriek. He awoke in an instant and the scream was repeated a few seconds later. The colonel leaped from his bed and ran to the door. He wrenched it open and rushed out into the corridor. Then he stopped dead. His daughter was standing a dozen feet to his left, along the passage. She was in her nightgown and as pale as could be. Little wonder, because an arm was clamped around her throat, which had the effect of hugging her close to the man who was standing behind her. It was Andrew Crawley.

'Don't you hurt her now,' said Farrance. 'You just let her go now and we will deal with this man to man. You hear what I tell you?'

Crawley's face was a mask of demonic triumph and it struck Colonel Farrance that the man looked as though he had lost his senses. He said to his daughter, 'Just keep calm, Charlotte. This man will not hurt you.'

'Well now, Bob,' said Crawley in a jovial voice, quite at odds with the desperate nature of the situation, 'you could not be more wrong about that.' He showed Farrance the pistol which he held in his right hand and placed the muzzle of it behind Charlotte's ear. 'I aim to blow out this child's brains and I got her to scream a little so that you would wake up and watch.'

Charlotte was almost fainting with fear and her knees were sagging. It was only Crawley's arm around her throat that was keeping her from slumping to the floor. Although his bowels were almost turning to water in terror at the thought of any harm befalling his child, Farrance thought that there was one last gamble worth trying. He said, 'Andrew, you do know that this is likely as not your daughter and not mine? She was born nine months after you stayed with me and Annie. Think on that.' Thankfully, Charlotte looked as though she had fainted altogether by this time and so was unlikely to have heard.

'The hell are you talking about?' asked Crawley in apparently genuine bewilderment. 'I never screwed your wife.'

'I saw you,' Farrance reminded him.

Crawley smiled wickedly. 'Oh, that. Yes, I saw you through the window, coming along the street like you hadn't a care in the world. I was going that day anyway and so thought I'd kind of leave you something to remember me by. I pulled down my pants and jumped on that wife of yours. She was struggling and crying out and then you walked through the door. Boy, your face was a picture!'

It was not the time to think this through; it was enough for the colonel to see that this line of appeal to Crawley's better nature was pointless. He aimed to hurt Farrance as bad as he could and the murder of his only child would surely be the best way to accomplish that end. It was at this moment that Colonel Farrance became aware of a figure moving stealthily along the passage and approaching Crawley and his daughter from behind. It was Ikey Wilson and he had had the foresight to pick up his Remington before leaving his bedroom; which was, by the by, more than Farrance had done.

The fear in Colonel Farrance's heart was that Crawley was a man with nothing left to lose. He was a fugitive who would hang for the murder of the deputy and so had chosen to exact this last terrible revenge upon the man he held to be ultimately responsible for his predicament. Did Wilson know this? If challenged or likely to be apprehended, then Crawley had nothing to lose by killing Charlotte; he could only hang once. Please God that Ikey had figured all this out and did not try to treat with the man like a reasonable being.

He need not have worried, because Ikey Wilson had worked out the odds of this drama as soon as he had heard Charlotte scream out in panic. His aim was simply to kill Andrew Crawley; not to parlay with him, offering him a safe passage or aught of that sort. He moved silently towards the little tableau of the vicious man holding the helpless and innocent young girl. Then he struck.

As soon as he was in reach of Crawley, Ikey Wilson's left hand snaked out and grabbed the wrist holding the gun to Charlotte's head. He gripped this with all his strength and jumped backwards, causing Crawley to loosen his grip on the child. At the same instant, Colonel Farrance jumped forward and caught the swooning girl before she fell to the floor. He picked her up and raced to his bedroom to put her out of danger. Pausing only to snatch up his own pistol, which was hanging from the gun belt which he had cast carelessly over the back of the chair, he went back into the corridor. Just as he reached the threshold, there came two shots, deafening in the narrow confines of the passageway outside his bedroom.

As he emerged into the corridor, lit only by the pale light of early dawn, Farrance saw that Ikey Wilson and Andrew Crawley were grappling with each other and that each appeared to be preventing the other from bringing up their guns to fire. He had a clear line of sight to Crawley and so did not hesitate to fire, the bullet taking Crawley in the throat and dropping him at once. 'You all right there, Ikey?'

he asked his old comrade.

'Not really, Bob,' came the reply. 'I think he has done for me.'

'Don't say so. Here, let me have a look there. You say you are shot?'

'Don't you trouble about me. How's Charlotte? Is she safe?'

'Yes, she's fine,' said Farrance. 'Hey, hold up man!' he said, as Wilson leaned unsteadily against the wall and then slid slowly to the floor. He went over and examined Ikey carefully, finding the wound in his chest at once.

'You're going to be all right, Ikey,' said the colonel. 'It is nothing. You and me both have had worse than that. It is a scratch. I am surprised to hear you make such a fuss over a little flesh wound; you must be getting old.'

'I am cold,' said Wilson. 'You best use that reward money yourself, Bob. Or give it to Charlotte, perhaps. I will have no use for it where I am going today.'

Feeling awkward, Farrance put his arm around Wilson's shoulders and said, 'Don't talk so, Ikey. You will be fine.'

It was in this attitude that Charlotte Farrance came out of the bedroom a quarter-hour later, after she had come to, and found the two men sitting together on the blood-soaked carpet. Right next to them was the dead body of the man who had threatened to kill her. She said to her father, 'Is Mr Wilson all right?'

'Not hardly,' came the reply. 'He is stone dead.'

The girl started to sob softly at these tidings and her father put his arm around her, relinquishing his hold upon the dead man, who then slumped sideways to the floor. This circumstance provoked a fresh paroxysm of grief from Charlotte, who clung to her father as though she were six and not sixteen. At length, her tears subsided and she said, 'Did he give up his life to save mine?'

'Well, I reckon that that is just what happened.'

'I liked him. He was funny and kind.'

'Which,' said Colonel Farrance, 'is by no means a bad epitaph.'

The repercussions of the deaths at the home of Whyteleafe's leading citizen were surprisingly muted and insignificant. The sheriff knew Colonel Farrance very well, both professionally and socially. He was inclined to treat the case as being a burglar disturbed in the night, who had seized a hostage to effect his escape. In the resulting struggle, the colonel's house guest had gallantly given up his life to save a young girl. It would have amused Ikey Wilson mightily to know that in death he became a law-abiding and heroic figure.

The reward for the breaking-up and capture of the best-organized gang of counterfeiters since the end of the war was a considerable one and, as Wilson had desired with his last dying breath, went to Charlotte. Colonel Farrance set up a trust fund, so that at the age of twenty-one, the money would be his daughter's, to do with as she wished.

The episode at Endeavour and its aftermath were by way of being a coda in the adventurous life of Robert Farrance; the last little bit of excitement before he settled down to spend the rest of his days in peace and quiet. With the deaths of Ikey Wilson and Andrew Crawley, the last connections with his life as an outlaw were severed and he was able to devote the remainder of his life to caring for his daughter and maintaining the character of a war hero and respected member of the community.